As Eagles Fly

Barbara Cartland

As Eagles Fly

THORNDIKE
CHIVERS

This Large Print edition is published by Thorndike Press®, Waterville, Maine USA and by BBC Audiobooks Ltd, Bath, England.

Published in 2006 in the U.S. by arrangement with Cartland Promotions.

Published in 2006 in the U.K. by arrangement with Cartland Promotions.

U.S.	Hardcover	0-7862-8417-X	(Candlelight)
U.K.	Hardcover	10: 1 4056 3757 9	(Chivers Large Print)
U.K.	Hardcover	13: 978 1 405 63757 2	
U.K.	Softcover	10: 1 4056 3758 7	(Camden Large Print)
U.K.	Softcover	13: 978 1 405 63758 9	

The text of this Large Print edition is unabridged.
Other aspects of the book may vary from the original edition.

Set in 16 pt. Plantin by Al Chase.

Printed in the United States on permanent paper.

British Library Cataloguing-in-Publication Data available

Library of Congress Cataloging-in-Publication Data

Cartland, Barbara, 1902–
    As eagles fly / by Barbara Cartland.
      p. cm. — (Thorndike Press large print Candlelight)
    ISBN 0-7862-8417-X (lg. print : hc : alk. paper)
    1. Muslims — Russia — Fiction.   2. Large type books.
  I. Title.   II. Thorndike Press large print Candlelight series.
PR6005.A765A9 2006
  823'.912—dc22   2005036114

As Eagles Fly

Author's Note

In 1801 the Kingdom of Georgia, situated between the Black Sea and the Caspian Sea, had been peacefully joined to the great Russian Empire.

But to the north, in the impenetrable snow-peaked Caucasian mountains there began a terrible Holy War which was to last until 1861.

Shamyl, Imam of Daghestan, the Shadow of Allah on earth, led the fanatical Moslem tribesmen who died rather than be taken alive.

Shamyl's son, aged eight, was captured during one battle and became a hostage, so the mystical leader of many legends brooded over his vengeance for thirteen years of bloodshed and bravery.

The hero and heroine of this story are fictitious, but the whole background and all the characters mentioned are authentic and part of history.

Shamyl was defeated and forced to surrender in 1859 but was treated kindly by the new Tzar, Alexander II.

Djemmal Eddin died after three years in the mountains, pining away for the life he had known and loved in St. Petersburg.

Chapter One

1855

The cavalcade wound round the steep side of a mountain.

The horses were picking their way on so narrow a rocky path that one slip and they and their riders would have been dashed to death in the valley thousands of feet below.

Led by the Murids, the fighting men with their black banners and black *tcherkesshas,* they were a colourful band in contrast with the clear brilliance of the deep snow.

Besides the Caucasians there were fifteen mounted servants with pack horses whom Lord Athelstan had brought with him on the journey.

It had been a long one as he had come to the Caucasus from Persia, where he had stayed with the Shah, and before that from India.

Riding at the head of his own staff, and behind the Caucasians who were leading the way, Lord Athelstan looked like a knight of old going into battle.

He was, perhaps, the one man from the Western world who did not by contrast look insignificant beside the *Dhighits* or Caucasian braves — the dashing young mountaineers who were considered the world's most handsome people.

Tall, dark, eagle-faced, with narrow waists and elegant hands and feet, they had an indefinable air of breeding, while their physique and stamina were the envy of their inveterate enemies — the Russians.

Lord Athelstan was heavier of build but he was outstandingly good-looking, and his breeding proclaimed itself in the manner in which he carried himself proudly, seeming to ignore the perilous path on which they were travelling.

There was in fact something so detached and reserved about him that it was almost as if he disdained to notice any physical perils and was completely concentrated on his thoughts.

"There are those who criticise his Lordship for his aloofness," the Foreign Secretary told the Queen, "but no-one can deny his reputation as a brilliant diplomat!"

He did not add that some women complained Lord Athelstan was cold but they were the women who tried in vain to entice him with their lips and with their bodies.

He could, if he wished, exert a charm that was irresistible. And there was no doubt that much of his diplomatic success was due to the manner in which Sultans, Shahs, Rulers of all sorts, could be persuaded to agree with him.

Even when, as a diplomat remarked, "It seemed impossible for them ever to find a mutual ground for negotiation!"

It seemed extraordinary that Lord Athelstan should already be so outstanding at the age of thirty-five and have risen so quickly to the almost unique position he now held.

But it was all actually done by tremendous will-power, a 'one-point' concentration on his objective, and a ruthless determination to let nothing stand in his way.

"Send for Athelstan" had become a familiar formula in the Foreign Office in London, but moving along the side of this mountain Lord Athelstan asked himself:

"Has any man ever had such a strange commission as my present one?"

He had been leaving India when he had received an urgent communication marked 'Secret and Confidential' ordering him to proceed to the Caucasus.

There he was told to interview Shamyl, Imam of Daghestan, the legendary leader who alone had prevented the Russians from dominating the last stronghold bordering their far-flung Empire.

It was a source of grave anxiety to England that Russia had expanded until she was now firmly established south to the Crimea, west to the Austro-Hungarian Empire, North and East to the boundaries of China.

"Only the Caucasus," Lord Athelstan had said in London, "with the impassable mountains of Daghestan, remains unconquered."

For the last twenty years, with enormous loss of life, the Russians had pitted their forces against one man.

That they had not been victorious with their superior weapons, their endless supply of recruits, and the best brains in the Russian Army, was due to the fact that they were not fighting an ordinary war.

"Shamyl, the Avar, the Imam of Daghestan, leads his men in a dedicated religious movement," Lord Athelstan was told. "Every man is a militant fanatic who resists the enemy, not only with fire and sword, but with his very soul."

The legends about Shamyl had grown up

until he had become a mythical figure worshipped by those who followed him as the true representative of Allah, admired by the outside world and even by the Russians themselves.

Lord Athelstan knew that one of the reasons for his being sent to interview Shamyl was to ascertain how long he could hold out against the continual onslaught of the Imperial Russian armies.

"It has become," the Dutch Ambassador to Teheran told him, "an obsession with the Tzar, Nicholas I, to destroy Shamyl and take the Caucasus."

From England's point of view, the Caucasus was a bastion to protect the gateway to India.

The English were already having a great deal of trouble in Afghanistan, most of it incited by the Russians who infiltrated amongst the tribesmen and caused continuous and bloody fighting on the North-West frontier.

"While Tzar Nicholas prays," the Ambassador continued, "that the Cross supersedes the Crescent and Jerusalem be restored to Christian hands, the English cannot believe that he has no designs on India."

It was therefore obviously in the British interests to foster resistance to Russia and to encourage the continuance of the Caucasus war.

"At the same time we have done very little to help them," Lord Athelstan remarked.

"The Caucasians have received nine cannon with 30,000 rounds, 150 revolvers and 3,400 rifles," the Ambassador said.

"Hardly enough material with which to wage a major war," Lord Athelstan replied cynically.

The British Ambassador sighed.

"Had England sent an army into Caucasus to reinforce him then we could have made Shamyl our ally."

"That was certainly a missed opportunity," Lord Athelstan agreed.

He thought now that it was unlikely that he would be able to do anything to assist the Imam. At the same time he had an insatiable curiosity about the man concerning whom there were so many fantastic legends.

The legends had started when in 1832 the Russians had made a desperate effort to wipe out the Caucasian resistance once and for all.

At the battle of Grimri sappers had blasted a foothold for the guns and the Russians had dragged their heavy artillery into range.

These demolished the walls of the fort in which Shamyl and 500 of his men had held out against 10,000 Russians.

The Murids had known they must surrender when finally the crumbling, burning walls collapsed around them, but they died fighting.

They came out to meet their enemy singly or in pairs, stepping forward slowly.

Then suddenly at close quarters they slashed out violently with their swords, each killing two or three Russians before being overpowered.

But one escaped — Shamyl.

With the spring of a wild beast, he leapt clear over the heads of the Russian soldiers about to fire on him. Landing behind them, he cut down three of them and was bayoneted by a fourth, the steel plunging deeply into his chest.

He seized the steel, pulled it out, cut down the man who had wounded him, and with another superhuman leap cleared a wall and vanished into the darkness.

The Russians were astounded, but they were sure that he must die of his wounds.

"The fight is over," they told themselves, "the Caucasus is won."

It was in fact to resist for another twenty-five years under the leadership of Allah's chosen mouth-piece on earth — his prophet Shamyl.

The Caucasians leading the way were now plunging down the side of what appeared to be a precipice without any footholds.

Yet the little Tchetchen horses seemed to move like flies over the rocky, black surface.

"No-one could behold the Caucasus," someone had said to Lord Athelstan before he left India, "and not feel the spirit of its sublime solitude awing his soul."

'It is certainly awe-inspiring,' he thought now.

The sombre, gloomy abysses, the wreaths of mist writhing serpent-like among the crevasses and gullies of the rocks, made it easy to believe that the Caucasian Djinns dwelt in these secret places.

Local legends were full of Djinns and Firies who lived high among the peaks, devil-like fierce creatures who held mysterious revels which resulted in sudden terrible storms and rushing winds.

But even without the legends, there was a mystery and a magic about the landscape.

High above everything towered the mountains, their sharp white peaks silhouetted against the sky. Now when the winter was nearly past, the first sign of spring was showing itself among clumps of giant plane trees and the reddish cliffs.

It had a beauty Lord Athelstan had never seen before in all his travels.

The heavy clouds clinging to the mountains seemed, at times, to close in on them in a menacing and possessive manner, at others to lift the mind to the sky so that it was hard to return to the slit defiles which revealed, five thousand feet below, torrents of crystal water raging over the rocks.

Sometimes he would see a tree-shrine clinging to a cliff face — a stunted thorn bush where the friars had attached a rag from their clothing to represent a prayer which would go on fluttering in the wind long after they had passed by.

They climbed and descended and climbed again until it seemed as if they moved in a world without time, without beginning or ending.

Then suddenly ahead of them Lord Athelstan saw Dargo-Vedin which was Shamyl's headquarters, the refuge he returned to between his battles.

He had chosen it because it was an almost inaccessible retreat which, as Lord Athelstan had already found, could only be reached by a terrifying journey along precipitous mountain paths.

The people spoke of it as the 'Great

Aôul', and as he had the first glimpse of the fortress surrounded by a stockade, a cavalcade of wild horsemen streamed out to meet him, their black banners flowing in the wind.

Behind Dargo-Vedin lay densely wooded slopes; in front of it there was a terrible ravine where, far below, an unbridged river raged across great boulders.

The horsemen, riding superbly, appeared to charge straight at Lord Athelstan, then reined in their horses at the last moment, which was in itself a salute of welcome.

They surrounded him and his party and led them with an air of triumph, towards their fortress.

There was only one entrance to it, defended by blockhouses and a watch tower from which there was a view over the whole countryside.

Looking round, Lord Athelstan could see one large gun of European make, a powder-magazine and what was obviously a store-house.

Beside it was a large water-tank, fed by a mountain stream, which had been diverted to fill the immense stone pool where, he was to learn later, both men and horses bathed.

He was, however, not allowed to stop but was led even further into Dargo-Vedin until he saw the Imam's own house built in the middle of an inner fortress.

It was guarded by his Murids with drawn swords.

Lord Athelstan dismounted and found a handsome, gaunt man, black-eyed and black-bearded, bowing before him.

"I am Hadjio, Your Excellency, Steward of the Imam. In his name I welcome you to Dargo-Vedin."

Lord Athelstan returned his greeting and was led into the house.

He noticed at once that it was very sparsely and austerely furnished. Then he was taken into the presence of the great Shamyl himself.

Seated on a plain wooden chair as if it were a throne, flanked by his Murids with drawn swords and an Interpreter, he was an extremely impressive figure.

Over six feet three inches tall, he had fine, chiseled features which proclaimed his noble descent. But it was believed locally that he was the son of a Georgian Prince.

With his henna-red beard, his strangely penetrating eyes under heavy eye-brows, he was the very embodiment of the mythical hero who would stir the imagination and arouse the adoration of his followers.

He always wore black and white, the

dashing classic clothes of the Caucasus.

His *tcherkessha,* a full-skirted, long, tight-waisted tunic, was barred across the chest with double rows of silver cartridge cases.

Ordinary Caucasians wore a heavy lambskin hat, but Shamyl's *papakh* was a gigantic red-tasselled turban edged with black lambswool.

His thin elegant feet were encased in supple black leather boots which were moulded to the ankle.

The palms of his hands, like his beard, were stained with henna.

For a moment the two men looked at each other.

The tall, proud, broad-shouldered Englishman with his cold reserve, and the fanatical leader of a Holy War which had resulted in the death of thousands of men, with his mystical aura of leadership.

Then Shamyl smiled.

"Welcome to Dargo-Vedin, Your Excellency. I must compliment you on your courage and tenacity in reaching us."

He spoke in his own dialect and Lord Athelstan, who had been studying the Tartar language ever since he left India, replied in the same tongue.

"I am extremely grateful for the opportunity of doing so."

"Few people dare or care to attempt the journey," Shamyl answered. "I can only hope that you will think it worthwhile."

"Whatever the outcome of our deliberations," Lord Athelstan replied, "the privilege of meeting the Imam is something I shall never forget."

Shamyl asked him to sit down and after Russian tea and the customary little cakes that went with it, the Imam asked for news from England, and what hope Lord Athelstan had brought him of aid from Queen Victoria.

It was hard to explain that the English, while anxious for the Caucasians to go on fighting, were not prepared to do anything practical or to supplement their contribution of weapons which Shamyl had already received.

Lord Athelstan had, however, brought a personal present for the Imam, a handsome gold watch and chain which seemed to please him.

The Murids liked time-pieces better than any other booty, and in any raid prized them more than jewellery.

Shamyl could not take the gift direct from Christian hands. Lord Athelstan placed it beside him on a table from which it was collected by a servant.

"My present to Your Excellency you will receive tomorrow," Shamyl explained. "It consists of two fine thoroughbred Kabarda stallions, which I am convinced you will find most useful on your return journey."

Lord Athelstan expressed his thanks and then he said a little tentatively:

"I was asked to enquire about the fate of your prisoners."

For a moment a shadow passed over Shamyl's face, before he replied:

"You have been told what happened?"

"I learnt when I was in India," Lord Athelstan replied, "that during a raid on Tzinondali you captured Her Serene Highness Princess Anna Tchavtchavada, her sister Princess Varvara, her niece Princess Nina, and a number of their children."

"That is correct," Shamyl answered. "And they are being held as hostages until my own son is returned to me."

Lord Athelstan was already aware that in 1839 Djemmal Eddin — Shamyl's son — had been handed over as a hostage after a battle in which, surrounded by overwhelming Russian forces, Shamyl had been obliged to surrender.

At the age of eight Djemmal Eddin had been taken to St. Petersburg, which had been not only a blow to Shamyl's pride as a leader, but a dagger-thrust to his love as a father.

He had plotted and planned, fought and suffered for thirteen years to find a way for his son to be returned to him. Now it appeared as if victory was within his grasp.

For seven months now he had held in Dargo-Vedin the Georgian princesses and their children while negotiations were proceeding to exchange them for Djemmal Eddin together with a ransom.

It was not Shamyl, Lord Athelstan knew, who was asking the exorbitant sum of one million roubles for the hostages, but his Murids who had grown greedy with the years.

They wanted the money to build up *aôuls* shattered by war and purchase new weapons with which they could go on fighting.

The capture of the Georgian princesses had caused a sensation throughout the world.

The fact that Christian women could be held captive by Moslems aroused the chivalry of men in every country.

Lord Athelstan, from his knowledge of Shamyl, was convinced that apart from acute discomfort the women would have come to no physical harm.

What he was certain Shamyl did not know was that his son, in the long years he had been in Russia, had become completely Westernised.

The Tzar, a cold remote figure both to his people who had never understood him and to the majority of aristocrats in St. Petersburg, had an affection for children.

He had taken the child, Djemmal Eddin, under his wing and supervised his upbringing.

Appointing himself Djemmal Eddin's guardian, the Tzar paid for all the expenses of his upbringing from his own purse and he had him brought to the Winter Palace several times a week.

He planned for Djemmal Eddin to enter the Cadet Corps with the sons of the Russian nobility, with the object of eventually obtaining a commission in one of the Guards Regiments.

Caucasian Princes who had sworn allegiance to Russia rather than to Shamyl were very popular at the Russian Court.

They were known as "furious eagles" and it is said that as they moved about the streets, the Court, the Ball-rooms and the Army headquarters of St. Petersburg, they had an "eagle glance and a light half-fleeting step that was peculiar to them."

Women found them irresistible.

Their horsemanship was fantastic. At full gallop standing in the stirrups, the reins held in their teeth, flourishing a *kindjal* and *shashka* in either hand, they would leap to the ground and back on to their horses.

Lord Athelstan had been in St. Petersburg only three years previously, when he had met Djemmal Eddin and realised that he had become not only the pet of the Tzar but of everyone at Court.

He was immensely popular.

His large, mournful, rather dark eyes above his high cheek bones, and his densely black, glossy hair made him outstanding even among the handsome, good-looking young Russians.

He rode magnificently; he spoke several languages; was musical; had studied astrology; and liked to paint.

What was more significant, Lord Athelstan thought, was that he seldom wore his native dress, not even the *tcherkessha* which made every Caucasian look so dashing.

He preferred to wear Russian uniform, and this was in fact a symbol of his conversion to the West.

Lord Athelstan wondered now if it was

possible to convey to Shamyl the fact that if Djemmal Eddin was brought back home in exchange for the Georgian Princesses, he would come reluctantly.

Then with his usual reserve, Lord Athelstan told himself it was none of his business.

He had merely been told to enquire after the health of the Princesses and to find out how soon the exchange was likely to be made. "We are at the moment at an *impasse*," Shamyl explained. "I understand that my son will be returned to me, but there is apparently some difficulty in raising the ransom money."

"Their Highnesses are in good health?" Lord Athelstan enquired.

"They are a part of my household," Shamyl replied.

"Would it be possible for me to see them?"

There was a moment's pause. Then Shamyl said:

"I wish to speak to Your Excellency on a private matter."

"I would deem it a privilege," Lord Athelstan replied.

Shamyl made a gesture with his hand and the Murids, with their drawn swords, and the Interpreter left the room, leaving the two men alone.

There was a little pause before Shamyl said:

"I would ask a favour."

"If it is possible the favour is already granted," Lord Athelstan replied, in the extravagant language of the East.

Shamyl hesitated and Lord Athelstan felt that he was finding difficulty in expressing himself. Then he said:

"Among those I hold as hostages there are two who were brought here unnecessarily."

Lord Athelstan raised his eye-brows and Shamyl went on:

"You will understand that my instructions were to bring everyone who was in the home of Prince David Tchavtchavadze. It was not possible for my men to distinguish between individuals."

"I understand," Lord Athelstan said.

"There was, for instance, a French governess, Mrs. Drancy, who has been nothing but a trouble to us."

There was a faint smile on Shamyl's lips as he spoke, and Lord Athelstan guessed that a voluble French woman would not behave with the same dignity or reserve as the Princesses.

"And also staying at Tzinondali was a friend of the Princess Nina, who is only seventeen and unmarried."

Lord Athelstan did not speak, wondering what Shamyl was about to reveal to him.

"Her name is Countess Natasha Melikov," Shamyl went on. "She and her young brother, aged nine, were conveyed here with the rest, although as hostages they have no significance."

"Why not?" Lord Athelstan enquired.

"They are orphans, and there is no-one, so they tell me, who would make any effort to ransom them," Shamyl answered.

"Surely they can return to Russia with the rest of your prisoners when the terms of exchange are agreed?" Lord Athelstan asked.

"My people are loath to part with two Russian aristocrats who cannot pay for their release," Shamyl said simply. "I have, therefore, to find a solution."

Lord Athelstan waited.

He had a feeling he was somehow bound up in all this, but he could not for the moment see how.

"The Countess Natasha is extremely attractive," Shamyl said. "In fact by most standards she is undoubtedly a great beauty. I have, therefore, with her agreement, arranged that she should become the wife of the Sultan Abdul Aziz."

"With her agreement?" Lord Athelstan questioned sharply.

"In exchange for which," Shamyl continued, "her brother, Prince Dimitri, will be exchanged with my other prisoners."

Lord Athelstan was too experienced a diplomat either to allow his feelings to show in his face or to be expressed hastily by his lips.

But he knew what the world outside would think of a Christian woman being sent as wife to the Sultan of Turkey — a Moslem who already had four wives and a notoriously large harem of concubines.

As if he knew what he was feeling, there was a faint smile on Shamyl's lips as he said:

"I am asking Your Excellency if you will escort this young woman to Constantinople, where I understand you will go to find a ship to carry you to England."

Lord Athelstan stiffened before he replied:

"You will understand that that is quite impossible. I am a Diplomat and I claim diplomatic immunity in every country I visit because I play no part in their politics, their intrigues and interfere in nothing except that which affects my own country."

He felt as if Shamyl did not understand the point he was making and went on:

"It would be inconceivable for me to take under my protection a woman whose action in agreeing to marry the Sultan would deeply offend the Russians through whose country I must pass when I leave here."

"I thought perhaps that would be your Excellency's attitude," Shamyl said, apparently quite unperturbed. "It was, in fact, the Countess herself who suggested it."

"You will please convey my regrets to the Countess," Lord Athelstan said coldly. "But there is nothing I can do in this matter, to oblige either you or her."

Shamyl nodded his head. Then he said:

"Your Excellency will realise it is quite a problem. My gift to the Sultan concerns me deeply because as a Moslem he has always given me his encouragement and good wishes."

He paused to continue:

"I would however, ask for something more substantial such as arms and men, if I am to continue to fight the Russians. It is not only in the interests of my own country but of Great Britain also."

"That is appreciated," Lord Athelstan agreed.

"It is of course also essential that my gift should arrive unharmed," Shamyl went on. "Apart from the insult to the lady in question if she should be violated on the way, she would on arrival at the Sultan's Palace be put to death by one of the less swift and certainly more painful methods of execution."

Lord Athelstan thought briefly of the Turkish method of death by strangulation, the manner in which badly behaved concubines were dropped into the Bosporus, and of unspeakable tortures which were often repeated and re-repeated amongst those who knew the East.

It only confirmed his conviction that this was a matter in which he could take no part.

"Again you must accept my apologies," he said quietly.

Shamyl did not reply.

He rose to his feet and the interview was at an end. Only as he withdrew from the room in which the audience had taken place did he say:

"We will meet again after sunset, Your Excellency, and I hope in the meantime you will think a little further on the subject we have just discussed."

He disappeared before Lord Athelstan could answer him, and Hadjio, the Steward, rejoined him to take him to his quarters where he was to sleep.

The room which he was allotted was small and contained only mats on the floor, with shelves around the room on which were piled rolls of bedding should he require it.

Lord Athelstan, however, always travelled with everything necessary for his own comfort.

His Major Domo, who had once been a Sergeant-Major in his Regiment, would, he was convinced, have managed to provide him with everything to which he was accustomed, even if they found themselves at the North Pole.

A bluff Englishman in appearance, Hawkins was, in fact, an extremely clever and astute man.

He spoke a number of foreign languages in the vernacular and he had methods of his own of making himself understood even in dialects which perplexed his master.

"What do you think of Dargo-Vedin?" Lord Athelstan asked him.

"Might as well settle down in an eagle's nest, M'Lord," Hawkins answered.

He glanced over his shoulder as if he thought someone might be listening, and then he went on in a low voice:

"From all I hear, M'Lord, these Caucasians won't be able to hold out much longer against them Russians."

"Why do you think that?" Lord Athelstan enquired.

He was, however, listening intently.

He relied on Hawkins, on journeys such

as this, to find out from native gossip and from his own observations as much, if not more, than he was able to do through the usual diplomatic channels.

"A great many of the Caucasians, M'Lord," Hawkins answered, "are deserting to the Russians. They want to be on the winning side."

"That was what I heard in Teheran," Lord Athelstan said. "Well, learn all you can, Hawkins. It is important, as you well know."

"I only hopes, M'Lord, that we're not staying long," Hawkins said with an air of disgust. "I never fancied heights, and I've not much to say for these mountaineers except they can ride."

He went from the room and Lord Athelstan smiled to himself. Hawkins was always the same.

He had a contempt for foreigners wherever he might find them, but many of Lord Athelstan's missions had been brought to a successful conclusion by the help of Hawkins.

Lord Athelstan ate alone because, whatever happened elsewhere, it was impossible in Shamyl's house for a Christian to sit down with a Moslem.

The tough lamb, the rice, a sparsity of

vegetables, hard goat's cheese and tea were what he might have expected and not even the most exciting conversation would have made them more palatable.

But he knew that the Caucasians ate very sparingly and could fight without the cumbersome supply-wagons with samovars of tea which were essential for the Russians.

Meat was a rarity for the Murids, and then only lamb, goat or chicken was permitted.

Cakes of roughly ground millet and goat's cheese formed their main diet, which sustained their incredible stamina and magnificent physique.

"During a campaign," a Russian General told Lord Athelstan, "these creatures will subsist on flowers or leaves and they consider rhododendrons very sustaining."

The tea with which Lord Athelstan was served was the kind generally used by the Caucasians. A heavy compote of tea-leaves was mixed with sheep's blood and formed into square bricks which dissolved when put into hot water.

Lord Athelstan was used to it and did not mind the somewhat pungent flavour, but he knew that Hawkins would grumble.

With the dark it was bitterly cold.

The snow-clad 'Mountain of Stais' towered over them and the wind made eerie sounds not unlike a banshee's wailing.

Lord Athelstan was waiting for a summons to join Shamyl when there was a knock on the door of his room.

"Come in," he said, and the door opened.

He turned, expecting to see a Murid with a drawn sword. But instead into the room came a woman, and when he looked at her he realised she was quite the most beautiful girl he had ever seen.

At first glance she appeared to be dressed in rags. Then he saw that what had once been a smart silk dress with a fashionably tight bodice and full skirts, had been torn, ripped and pulled until there was hardly an inch of it which was not stitched and darned.

The effect of this, combined with the fact that the material was discoloured by exposure to the elements, was to give the appearance of a beggar.

Lord Athelstan realised that the hostages must have no clothes other than those they stood up in when they had been kidnapped from the house in the country.

He was well aware what their journey must have been like before they reached Dargo-Vedin and he had already heard that they had had to walk most of the way.

But even her ragged dress could not detract from the beauty of the girl who faced him.

She carried herself superbly, was taller than any Moslem woman, and had the gazelle-like grace of the Russian aristocrats.

Her face was a perfect oval but, because she was so emaciated by the deprivations of the last few months, her eyes seemed to fill her whole face.

Huge, dark eyes, full of Slav mystery, they stared at Lord Athelstan enquiringly as if she scrutinised him and summed up everything she saw.

For a moment neither of them spoke, and then the girl said in English:

"I am Natasha Melikov. I wish to talk to Your Excellency."

"It will be an honour," Lord Athelstan said. "Will you sit down?"

He indicated a pile of soft cushions which had been in his baggage and were covered with a rich silk brocade.

"Thank you," the Countess said, inclining her head.

She seated herself and Lord Athelstan did likewise.

She noticed as he did so that he was one of the few Western men she had ever met who could sit gracefully and with dignity on Eastern cushions.

Most Europeans felt it an indignity to sit so low; they were not certain what to do with their feet, and because they were embarrassed they hunched their backs.

Lord Athelstan sat upright, his hands on his knees, and he might, in fact, have been Shamyl himself granting an audience with an almost Royal condescension.

"I think you know why I am here," the Countess Natasha began.

"The Imam has already spoken of his desire that you should become the bride of the Sultan," Lord Athelstan replied. "I am sure you do not wish to hear my opinions on the matter."

"It is important that I should reach Constantinople," the Countess said, "and there is no way of my doing so if you will not take me."

"I have already informed the Imam that such a suggestion is impossible," Lord Athelstan replied. "As a Diplomat I cannot involve myself in the intrigues of those whose country I visit."

"These are somewhat exceptional circumstances," Countess Natasha said slowly. "Your Excellency knows as well as I do that it will be impossible for the Imam's men to escort me through Georgia. If my brother is to go free I have to find some way of reaching Constantinople."

"There must be, surely, less drastic methods of ensuring his release," Lord Athelstan suggested.

An expression of anger made Countess Natasha's eyes seem to flash as she answered:

"You cannot be so obtuse as not to realise I have considered every other method of escape from this prison. But it happens to be the only possibility open to me."

"I am deeply sorry for you," Lord Athelstan said. "I will be honest and say that the idea of your becoming the wife, which I imagine is a polite word for your future position, of the Sultan disgusts me, but I cannot help you."

"Do you realise what the alternative is?" the Countess asked in a low voice.

"No."

"Then I will tell you. I shall be left here when the others leave. If I am fortunate, I shall be married to a Naib — one of Shamyl's officers. His sons already have their full complement of wives, and as you must know, no woman is allowed to remained unmarried under the Imam's jurisdiction."

Her voice sharpened as she went on:

"Every widow must be remarried within

three months. It ensures, of course, a continuance of Caucasians to go on fighting against my country."

There was a pause and then she said:

"If I cannot marry an officer, then I shall just be offered to the first Murid who fancies me. As far as I am concerned it will just be a question of how quickly I can kill myself."

Lord Athelstan rose to his feet.

"This is preposterous!" he exclaimed. "Surely this cannot happen?"

"Are you so ignorant as not to realise it has happened a thousand times before?" Countess Natasha asked contemptuously. "We are not the first women who have been brought to Dargo-Vedin. We just happen to be the most important and therefore a commodity with which the Imam can bargain for the release of his son."

"I wish I could help you," Lord Athelstan murmured.

"I have told you what will happen to me," Countess Natasha said, "but there is also my brother, Count Dimitri, to be considered."

Lord Athelstan did not reply and she continued:

"He is nearly nine. After a few years here he will forget his own country and he will become a Caucasian. He will be taught the horsemanship and the other skills at which they excel, and then he will fight against his own people."

She drew in her breath and went on:

"Make no mistake, he will not be given a choice. Once he is of the right age he will fight or die."

Lord Athelstan sat down again on the cushions from which he had risen.

"I think both alternatives are appalling," he said, "but they are your problem and not mine."

"Are you afraid to take me with you?" Countess Natasha asked contemptuously. "I could be well disguised. I assure you that the Russians whom you meet in Georgia would never for one moment guess my identity."

"That is not the point," Lord Athelstan said.

"I think it is," the Countess Natasha contradicted. "I never thought to meet an Englishman who was a coward."

Lord Athelstan gave a little laugh with no humour in it.

"You are very cleverly trying to provoke me, Countess," he said. "You know as well as I do that nothing is likely to incite a man more than an accusation of cowardice. But may I tell you that it is often more difficult and courageous to refuse a request than to acquiesce in it. That is my position at the moment."

"You are really refusing me?" she enquired in a low voice.

"I am telling you that what you ask of me is impossible," he said. "It would involve a violation of the diplomatic privilege I am accorded everywhere I go. I cannot express my own feelings in this matter, I can only act correctly within the terms of my office."

The Countess rose to her feet.

"Is that your last word on the matter?"

"With the deepest regret, I can only reiterate that there is nothing I can do to help you."

He paused.

"I will, of course, speak to the Imam on your behalf, although I doubt if he will listen to me."

"It is the Murids who will not listen," Countess Natasha said bitterly. "Shamyl is a just man in his own way, but they have become greedy. The Holy War they have fought for so long and the Paradise for which they will die so willingly, pales beside the thought of golden roubles. They want to buy guns and more guns with which to go on killing."

Her voice seemed to ring out in the small

room. Then she looked at Lord Athelstan and he saw not only anger in her eyes, but a hatred that was almost like a glint of fire.

"You may be an excellent Diplomat, My Lord," she said, "but as a man I despise you."

Lord Athelstan's face was quite impassive, as he bowed to her almost ironically.

Holding her head high, with a dignity that was unmistakable, she swept by him.

He thought for a moment that her ragged dress might have been trimmed with ermine, and that she wore a coronet on her dark hair.

Chapter Two

Lord Athelstan stood for a long time after Countess Natasha had left the room wondering what he could do to help her.

He knew there was in fact nothing.

It was unthinkable that he should in his position get himself involved in anything so completely alien to Western thought.

When the Princesses returned to their homes, they would certainly relate what had happened to their friend, the young Countess, and the whole world would be shocked at the thought of a Christian woman being incarcerated in the Sultan's Palace.

Every instinct in Lord Athelstan's body urged him to prevent this happening, but his mind told him logically and unemotionally that he was in fact powerless.

He could of course appeal to the Imam, and this he intended to do.

Hadjio came to tell him that his presence was required in the Selamek or Reception

Room, and putting on a thick cloak lined with sable, Lord Athelstan followed the Steward along the narrow, twisting passages of the Aôul.

As he went, he thought how bitterly cold the hostages must have found their prison after the warmth of their Palaces, which were kept so hot that gardens of flowers and orange trees bloomed inside them all the year round.

The Imam was waiting for Lord Athelstan, attended by only an Interpreter which, since His Lordship could speak to him in his own language, was only a formality.

They bowed to each other and exchanged the flowery, fulsome greetings which were usual in the East, before the Imam sent the Interpreter away so that they could sit alone over their cups of coffee.

It was then that Shamyl asked Lord Athelstan to tell him the truth as to the prospect of his receiving any help from England in his fight against the Russians.

Choosing his words with care, Lord Athelstan was truthful.

He knew as he spoke that what he had to say was in fact what the Imam had expected, even though it was bitter for him to realise that he must go on alone or be conquered.

Things in the Caucasus had, Lord Athelstan learnt, been far more difficult since Field-Marshal Prince Alexander Bariatinsky had taken command of the Russian troops.

Four years earlier, in 1851, he had begun to win battle after battle against Shamyl's forces.

His methods were entirely different from those used by any previous Commander. By a series of out-flanking manoeuvres, new to Shamyl's forces — whereas before head-on battles had been usual — he was able to gain successes which were astonishing.

He used methods very unlike those employed by the Russians in the past, and he had a sense of theatre and drama which almost equalled Shamyl's.

After one battle, when there had been terrible fighting on both sides, he accepted the surrender of a large body of Tchetchens. He then gave them back their swords, dismissed his own men and told the Tchetchens to guard him while he slept.

These new methods, combined with a clemency never known before, impressed the Caucasians and resulted in quite a number of minor tribes defecting to the Russian side.

Prince Bariatinsky even changed the landscape itself.

The great forests had always been Shamyl's finest natural defence, so much so that not only did he impose very heavy fines on any man cutting down a tree for his own purposes but he often hanged offenders there and then as a warning to others.

Prince Bariatinsky felled the forests, cleared the scrub and bridged the rivers.

From high in the mountains Shamyl with his telescope fixed on the woodcutters, could watch his defences falling one by one, and knew there was nothing he could do about it.

Looking at the Imam sitting opposite him, remembering the legends of his invincibility, Lord Athelstan could not help feeling sadly that Shamyl was nearing the end of the road.

The Russians would never give up, and they were encroaching nearer and nearer to Dargo-Vedin, his secret stronghold which, as Hawkins said, was like an eagle's nest, but which one day he might have to surrender.

There was, however, the present to contend with and this included the hostages who if rumour was to be believed, were very near their time of release.

Shamyl had an amazing chain of communication, which kept him to a large extent in touch with the outside world.

He had set it up soon after he came to power, having admired the system employed by the Russians of posting along their military highways.

But Shamyl used a relay system across country where no foreigner could go, over glaciers, forests, swamps and mountains.

The swift Caucasian horses were the link in the chain by which news could be transmitted at an almost incredible speed.

Every aôul under his command kept in readiness their fastest horses, saddled and ready for a messenger who might arrive at any moment by day or night on an exhausted mount.

If the man was ill, if he was wounded or otherwise unable to travel further, another rider was ready in a second to carry on the messages.

The Caucasians rode in every type of weather, crossed raging torrents, clung to the perilous paths to reach Shamyl, carrying despatches which told him every detail of Russian life.

He knew not only of reinforcements and the arrival of new Regiments and more guns, but also of balls and the gossip of Society; of which particular Circassian beauty was the mistress of which officer; of talks with local Khans and who was acting as a spy against him.

Shamyl was in fact far better informed than his enemies.

Their paid spies were found dead at night with a knife in their backs; their new offensives were anticipated and their element of surprise ineffective.

Lord Athelstan therefore suspected that Shamyl was well aware that his son, Djemmal Eddin, had left St. Petersburg in January and had driven in a troika, accompanied by an escort of Cossacks, to Moscow.

There he was fêted. Balls were given in his honour and he was fawned on by all the most beautiful women in Moscow.

At the beginning of February he should have reached Vladikavkaz where the Russians would undoubtedly treat him as a hero.

Shamyl did not tell Lord Athelstan all he knew, but from long years of trying to fathom the twisted tangles of the Eastern mind and having seen Djemmal Eddin in St. Petersburg, Lord Athelstan could fill in a lot that remained unsaid.

He realised it had been a stab in the heart

to Shamyl when his son was taken from him.

But he wondered if he would not experience an even greater agony when the same son returned radically changed and now completely alien to what must seem to him a barbarian existence.

It was, however, impossible for Lord Athelstan not to admire the Imam and to know that, when history came to be written, he would go down as one of the great leaders of the world and a great Visionary.

They talked for a long time.

Lord Athelstan at last expressed the thoughts that were uppermost in his mind:

"I have seen the Countess Natasha," he said. "Would it not be possible to allow the lady and her small brother to go free?"

"Without recompense?" Shamyl asked.

"Why not?" Lord Athelstan asked. "You were not expecting a ransom for them when they were captured."

"That is true," Shamyl answered. "At the same time I have many prisoners, some of whom have been held in Dargo-Vedin and in other parts of my territory for more than ten years. What will I say to them if for no apparent reason two aristocrats, who have been my prisoners for little over seven months, are returned without payment?"

It was a logical answer to which Lord Athelstan knew there was no reply.

He was well aware of the sufferings endured by the prisoners of the Caucasians.

There must, he thought, be hundreds of other Georgian captives, soldiers and people of no consequence, who would never be ransomed and therefore would die where they were incarcerated in the small, cold, airless prisons where they were half-starved and where terrible tortures were often inflicted on them.

"It is not my decision alone," Shamyl said after a moment. "My Murids would not tolerate it."

This Lord Athelstan knew was true. Things had changed in the Caucasus since Shamyl had tried to unite the whole country against the common enemy.

The Murids had grown more powerful and they were not prepared to accept the ideal of a Holy War without more material recompense.

They had become avaricious, and at this very moment they were over-ruling the Imam on the amount that should be paid for the Princesses.

A little later when Shamyl had left him, Lord Athelstan was to learn of this from Princess Anna.

He asked again if he might see the hostages and he knew it was only with reluctance that Shamyl finally agreed that he should talk for a few minutes with Princess Anna.

Thinking about her while he waited in the Selamek, Lord Athelstan remembered meeting her once some years ago when he had first visited Georgia.

The grand-daughters of George XII, the last King of Georgia, Her Serene Highness Princess Anna and her younger sister Princess Varvara were outstandingly beautiful in a country of beautiful women.

They had both been appointed Lady-in-Waiting to the Tzarina and after being admired and courted in St. Petersburg Society, they had married two handsome Georgian princes and returned to live in their own country.

As he waited Lord Athelstan wondered if Princess Anna's looks had been impaired by what she had suffered.

He could not imagine anything more distressing than for a gently nurtured lady, used to all the comfort and luxury that money could buy, to be imprisoned in this cold, bare, frightening, mountain stronghold.

But when the Princess Anna came into

the room, he realised that apart from appearing ill and very thin, she had not really altered.

Her classical features were still perfect, her thick black hair was coiled into a chignon on her proud head, and she looked just as statuesquely regal in the tattered rags that she wore as she had been in a ball-gown and fabulous jewels when Lord Athelstan had last seen her.

She held out her hand with a little cry of welcome, and he raised her fingers to his lips.

She was accompanied into the room by two Murids with drawn swords and the Interpreter who, Lord Athelstan knew, would repeat every word and even the intonation of their voices, to Shamyl.

"Your Serene Highness is all right?" Lord Athelstan asked in English.

"We are alive," Princess Anna replied.

"I will not waste time in expressing my sorrow at what has happened to you," Lord Athelstan said. "I know what you must have suffered, and I can only pray that your captivity is now at an end."

"That is what we are praying for," Princess Anna answered, "but I am desperately afraid that something will happen at the last moment to prevent our release."

"The ransom?" Lord Athelstan asked.

"Exactly," she answered. "It is impossible to convince these people that my husband cannot raise a larger sum. He has already offered 40,000 roubles. They say it is not enough."

There was an agony in the Princess's voice and Lord Athelstan said quickly:

"I am sure in the end it will be acceptable. The Imam's only thought for the last thirteen years has been that he should have his son returned to him."

"That is our one hope," Princess Anna answered, "but I cannot help feeling sorry for Djemmal Eddin."

"You know him?" Lord Athelstan asked.

"Very well indeed. He is a charming, delightful boy. Very cultured, and I know that he has almost forgotten his home. He is Russian through and through. How will he ever endure this life?"

It was typical, Lord Athelstan thought, that Princess Anna, who was a remarkable character, should think of Djemmal Eddin's sufferings in the midst of her own.

Then she said with a sigh:

"I am not only thinking of myself if we are not rescued, but of the children. How can they remain here to be brought up as Caucasians, the girls married off when they are

almost too young to know what is happening to them; the boys taught to fight
against our own people?"

"I am sure what your husband has offered
will be acceptable," Lord Athelstan said
soothingly. "You know as well as I do that
they are bound to bargain, to argue and to
try to extract a little more up to the very last
moment."

Princess Anna sighed.

"I try to cheer myself up by thinking that,
but you can imagine what it has been like
these last months."

"Has your treatment been very harsh?"
Lord Athelstan asked.

"No," she answered. "Shamyl is a just
man, but Your Lordship will appreciate he
cannot always control his household, and
women are always more spiteful than
men."

Lord Athelstan guessed that she must
have suffered at the hands of Shamyl's
wives.

"At first it was terrible," Princess Anna
went on in a low voice. "There were twenty-
three of us all in one small room and not allowed to move out of it. Later our servants
were given separate accommodation."

There was a brooding look on her face as
if she were remembering how intolerable

the situation had been. Then with a smile she went on:

"Only the children did not mind, and Shamyl has always been kind to them. Every day he has them brought to his room where he plays with them, giving them fruit and lollipops."

"It seems hard to imagine," Lord Athelstan remarked.

"It is true," Princess Anna said. "No matter how many problems he has on his mind, or how concerned he is with his wars, he always has time for the children."

"It is something I certainly did not expect to hear," Lord Athelstan remarked.

"When my baby Alexander was ill, the Imam fetched medicine men from his farthest provinces," Princess Anna went on. "He even had him wrapped in the skin of a freshly-slaughtered sheep which the Caucasians regard as an infallible cure."

"The child is alive?" Lord Athelstan asked gently.

"Shamyl gave permission for him to sleep with a Nurse outside our crowded room which had been weakening him," Princess Anna answered, "and after that he began to mend slowly."

"I am glad."

It was strange, Lord Athelstan thought,

that two men who hated each other, whose life work had been to oppose each other, Shamyl and the Tzar, were both so fond of children.

Perhaps if they ever met, children might become a mutual bond to foster some understanding between them.

Then as if she realised time was passing and she would not be able to linger with Lord Athelstan, Princess Anna said:

"I would speak to you about Natasha Melikov."

"I have already seen the countess," Lord Athelstan said. "I cannot help her."

"It is not possible for you to think of some way?" Princess Anna pleaded. "The Imam will not let her leave with us."

"He has already told me so."

"If she stays here her brother stays with her. If she goes to Constantinople as Shamyl intends, we can take Prince Dimitri home."

"I understand the problem," Lord Athelstan said, "but I regret it is utterly and completely impossible for me to be of assistance."

He thought the Princess Anna might be annoyed with him, but instead she smiled.

"I knew that would be your answer long before it was suggested," she said. "Here it is easy to forget the protocol that is so important in our previous lives."

"Thank you for understanding," Lord Athelstan said.

"I knew that as a Diplomat you could not stoop to intrigue," Princess Anna went on. "Natasha is too young to understand."

"I can only repeat how sorry I am to be so unhelpful," Lord Athelstan said.

"It is time to go," the Interpreter interrupted sharply.

Princess Anna held out her hand to Lord Athelstan. He took it and raised it to his lips.

"I am hoping that next time we meet it will be in very different surroundings."

"You have given me hope," Princess Anna replied, "not only by what you have said but just by my seeing you. Thank you."

Lord Athelstan kissed her hand again and then she was escorted from the room, while the Interpreter scurried away to relate to the Imam exactly what had been said, with doubtless some elaborations of his own.

Lord Athelstan would have gone back to his own room but Hadjio, the Steward, came to tell him that a feast had been arranged for his men and he wondered if His Lordship would be interested in seeing the dancing.

"We have few visitors," Hadjio explained,

"and tonight therefore, is an occasion for re-joicing amongst our people, who because they are not fighting men, never leave Dargo-Vedin."

Lord Athelstan did not say he could not imagine a worse fate, but he thought it. Wrapping his fur-lined cloak around him, he followed the Steward into one of the outside courtyards.

He knew Shamyl would not attend such a function, nor would his wives be allowed to do so, but it seemed as if everyone else in Dargo-Vedin was there. A small space in the centre had been left for the dancers.

There were torches of tarred wood which flared high into the clear mountain air and flickered on dark faces and flashing black eyes beneath black sheep-skin *papakhs.*

It was seldom that Shamyl's Murids had time for entertainment other than that of fighting and killing, and Lord Athelstan could feel an atmosphere of excitement which seemed to throb like the music as they waited for the dancers.

Caucasian music was usually sung to the accompaniment of *duduks,* which were reeded pipes, and a three-stringed *cithern* which had a plaintive sound that was somehow in keeping with the mystery of the mountains.

And there was a drum-beat, monotonous and hypnotic, which was, as Lord Athelstan knew, part of the leaping, wild, violent sword-dances which would later be performed by the warriors.

Now as he seated himself in the chair of honour, women sidled shyly into the centre of the courtyard to begin a *lesghinka.*

The dancers had long flowing sleeves with which to shield their faces besides the inevitable veils.

The *lesghinka* was a dance of conquest and of mating. It started slowly, the dancers moving almost reluctantly until when the rhythm quickened and the drums began their furious passionate beat, the women were joined by the men.

They circled around them, hemming them in, advancing as they retreated.

It was strange to watch, the light from the torches glinting on the daggers in the belts of the dancers, and to see their eyes flashing lustfully and to sense a response in the kohl-encircled eyes revealed above the evermoving veils.

All folk dances were made to excite, to titillate and to evoke desire. Lord Athelstan, glancing at the intent concentration of the spectators, knew that in this the *lesghinka* was successful.

He applauded and only when the sword-dances began did he return to his room.

There long after he was asleep, the beat of the drum still continued and the sharp cry of the warriors as they grew more excited and more abandoned rang out in the darkness.

Lord Athelstan, however, was tired and he slept well.

In the morning he was woken early by Hawkins.

"Did you enjoy yourself last night at the dancing?" Lord Athelstan asked.

"I've seen better, M'Lord," Hawkins replied grudgingly.

"Did you learn anything of interest?"

"Only what I told you before, M'Lord, that the Imam is losing many of his followers. In my opinion it is only a question of time before the Russians win."

This only confirmed what Lord Athelstan had thought himself and in a way he could not help feeling sorry.

For over twenty years the incredible Shamyl had held the Russians at bay and had forced them to expend men, guns and energy on the Caucasus — resources which might have been utilised elsewhere to England's disadvantage.

From the English point of view Shamyl

had been an asset, even though they had done nothing to help him.

To the Russians he was a continual thorn in the flesh, and Lord Athelstan wondered what mercy they would show him once he was completely defeated.

It was, however, time to go.

He made his formal farewells to the Imam who said that as a great mark of honour he personally would lead them part of the way.

Lord Athelstan knew that the Imam was still hoping almost against hope for help from England, but he accepted the gesture with some well-chosen words.

Then they all repaired to the courtyard where the horses were waiting.

As always, Shamyl was simply dressed in black, but his horse was caparisoned in crimson leather.

The whole Seraglio gathered in the court-yard to see them off and for the first time Lord Athelstan saw the children of Princess Anna and her sister, the little Tchavtchavadzes running around Shamyl, talking to him in some language that they both appeared to understand and making a nuisance of themselves under the horses' hooves.

The Imam swung himself into the saddle, and then, setting his horse at the gate ahead, started off at a gallop.

Lord Athelstan saw that the Great Aôul was surrounded by three separate walls. In each was a low portal, barely high enough for a rider to pass through it even when he bent low over his horse's neck.

The Imam never slackened his pace. As he approached each gate he swung himself low over his horse's side and at once rose again to stand up in the stirrups, flinging himself down again only a split second before the next gate.

It was the most dashing display of horsemanship Lord Athelstan had ever seen and he watched almost open-mouthed, as did the rest of the people.

Then they rode away encircled by the Murids, their black banners streaming from their lances, their war-like cries being swept away from their lips by the violence of the wind.

Once again after they had left Shamyl, there were the frightening cliffs to descend, the ravines to traverse, the cascades to cross.

It was a repetition of the hardships they had suffered on their way to Dargo-Vedin as they slithered down thousands of feet and climbed again up what appeared an impregnable precipice to reach a path hardly wider than a sheep track winding along the mountain side.

As the day progressed a faint sun appeared, the wind dropped and it became warmer.

Now they were going South-West and Lord Athelstan thought with pleasure that in Georgia the spring would have come, the snows would have melted.

It was only high in the Caucasus that the winter winds seemed to linger longer than anywhere else and he wondered why the Princesses had not died in their prison with the sheer cold of the dark winter nights.

If Russia was a land of extremes, so was the Caucasus, although it was difficult to compare the two in his mind when he thought of the strange, unpredictable, extravagant land to which the Princesses owed not only their breeding but their courage.

Nothing they had ever known however, could have prepared them for what they had to endure in Dargo-Vedin.

Just as Russia must have struck the young Djemmal Eddin as a fantastic fairy land of marvels, so in retrospect to the Princesses it must have seemed a lost Paradise.

Who could describe to Shamyl, who had never left the Caucasus, the beauty of the great Palaces in St. Petersburg or the splendour of the Court Balls which had over-whelmed even the most cosmopolitan of Europeans?

Lord Athelstan could remember the gigantic chandeliers lit with a thousand candles, in rooms festooned with garlands of hot-house flowers.

He could recall the glitter of the enormous mirrors which lined the walls between marble colonnades of rose, sulphur yellow or deep crimson.

Had Shamyl ever seen anything like the colossal urns of malachite and lapis lazuli or the heavily gilded furniture upholstered in silk?

Could he visualise the Princesses when they had waited on the Empress in the traditional Court dress of velvet with ermine-trimmed trains, wearing jewels of such value and such splendour they seemed too heavy for the long swanlike necks which were among their most beautiful characteristics?

In a short while they will be back in the world they know, Lord Athelstan reminded himself, and then they will forget all they have suffered.

Yet he was certain that anyone with as much character as Princess Anna would bear the scars of what she had undergone for the rest of her life.

And what of the Countess Natasha?

He found himself shying away from the question, unwilling to think of her problem or to try and decide in his own mind what was best for her.

Was it to be a lifetime in the Caucasus with one of the semi-barbarous, handsome but uncivilised Naibs or to be incarcerated in the over-scented luxury of the Sultan's harem, never again to speak with anyone of intelligence, and to live a life of utter stagnation?

It was not the physical terror of what awaited her which would be so hard to endure, but the fact that not only could her body become fat and soft without exercise, but her mind also would deteriorate.

All aristocratic Russians were highly educated. It was fashionable to have English nannies and French tutors. And being used to their own complicated language, the Russian children found everyone else's easy to learn.

What was more, all the Arts were encouraged and fostered in St. Petersburg.

It was almost impossible for a Russian girl of rank to be brought up as ignorant as her English counterpart was allowed to be.

Everyone from the Emperor and Empress

downwards attended the opera and the theatres. Poets, historians, authors, artists were welcomed and lionised.

For the men there was every kind of sport, and for the women, clothes and jewels beyond the dreams of even the most extravagant European Court.

The Russian temperament could never do things by halves, and that was why, Lord Athelstan told himself, it was possible to swing from the austerity, piety and fanatical dedication of Shamyl, to the eccentricities of those who served the Tzar.

It was typical that Shamyl had left his distinguished prisoners in the rags in which they arrived, and equally typical that the Empress Elizabeth had owned fifteen thousand dresses.

He remembered when he was in St. Petersburg hearing how wealthy Nobles sent their bailiffs to Dresden or Sèvres to purchase huge dinner services.

When they had been laboriously brought to Russia by wagon, there would be a gigantic feast and after it the dinner service would be used as a target for a shooting contest.

Who could explain Russia or understand it?

Lord Athelstan recalled that Countess

Saltikov's favourite hairdresser had been kept in a cage in case he should be tempted to work for anyone else.

The great Russian houses were staffed with an incredible number of servants. Countess Orlov, for instance, had eight hundred and always complained she could never get any tea when she wanted it.

It was all wildly incredible, just as he thought it would be hard to convince people of the difficulties he had encountered in reaching Dargo-Vedin or the life the great Imam lived as half warrior, half Prophet.

They pitched their tents the first night after leaving the Great Aôul in the shelter of some plane trees growing beneath a gigantically high mountain.

A meal was prepared for Lord Athelstan by his own servants and it was very much more appetising than the one he had eaten as a guest of the Imam.

When it was finished he slept on his own soft mattress filled with goose-feathers, with its silk-covered cushions, and fell asleep instantly.

He slept dreamlessly and awoke with the feeling of anticipation of what lay ahead.

To-day, although it would be a long march, they would leave the Caucasus and reach the boundaries of Georgia.

He was looking forward to staying with the Viceroy of the Tzar in Georgia as had been previously arranged, and he knew that when he had time he must set down in a report for the Foreign Office his impressions of Shamyl.

The Kabarda stallions which the Imam had presented to him were a gift Lord Athelstan greatly appreciated; in England he had a fine stable and was considered an excellent judge of horse-flesh.

He decided to ride one and told Hawkins to have his saddle transferred from his own horse to his new acquisition.

When he came from his tent Lord Athelstan found the Murids were waiting for him, the sun glinting on their silver knives.

As they saluted him he thought once again how handsome they were. He could understand that a great number of people looked on them as demi-gods.

As they moved off, leaving some of Lord Athelstan's servants to dismantle his tent, the Murids vied with each other in horsemanship.

They swung under the belly of their mounts, stood up in the saddle, rode with the reins in their teeth and took incredibly dangerous risks although the ground was uneven and it was easy to stumble inadvertently into a crevasse.

But it was all very good-humoured and when the first exuberance had quietened down, Lord Athelstan talked to many of the men, finding out if they enjoyed life that consisted of little except fighting and killing, and riding away to fight again the next day.

As he well knew, the pulse of Caucasian life was a battle, and if they had been offered any other sort of life they would not have appreciated it.

Lord Athelstan stopped briefly to eat and to water the horses and then pushed on again.

It was only when it was growing late in the afternoon and the light was fading, that they came round the side of a mountain to see ahead of them the lush, rolling plains of Georgia.

There was a distance of about three miles before they actually crossed the frontier and the Murids drew their horses to a standstill.

"This is where we say good-bye, Your Excellency," the Naib who was in charge said.

"Then I must thank you for your care of me," Lord Athelstan replied. "I am exceedingly grateful."

He gave the Naib a small time piece as a

present and a purse of money to be distributed amongst the men, which he knew would be appreciated.

Then with many exchanges of goodwill, the Caucasians turned and galloped away into the dusk. One moment their black banners were dark against the snow, the next — such was the speed at which they travelled — they were out of sight.

"We will go down into the valley," Lord Athelstan said to Hawkins, "and camp for the night."

"Very good, M'Lord."

Hawkins relayed the instructions in a variety of languages to Lord Athelstan's own staff.

They were men of many different nationalities whom Hawkins had picked up on their travels, choosing them only because they would be loyal, strong and trustworthy, and quite regardless of their colour or creed.

Lord Athelstan never questioned Hawkins' decisions; he had an instinct for choosing the right men.

Never once in all the difficulties in which Lord Athelstan had found himself had he ever been let down by his servants.

He rode ahead now, thinking that tomorrow night he would be in Tiflis and sleeping in a comfortable bed.

It never worried him to live rough, but at the same time he did not believe in discomfort for discomfort's sake, but only as a means to an end.

What was more, he was looking forward to meeting Prince Voronzov, the Viceroy, again, a man for whom he had a great admiration and who lived in enormous state. After the Imperial family, the Voronzovs were the first in Russia.

The last three miles down the hill was hard going, the terrain was rocky and treacherous, the horses were tired.

It had been a very long two days and though Lord Athelstan would not have admitted it, he too was feeling slightly fatigued.

He had enormous strength and great stamina, but the cold winds which never stopped blowing were as hard to endure as an incessant noise might have been, and at the moment he was also hungry.

Finally when they reached the lower land and found the flat plateau on which they could encamp, there was just enough light left for the servants to pitch the tents which had been carried on the back of the pack-horses.

Lord Athelstan's tent was particularly luxurious. It was made to be almost completely weatherproof. There was a Persian carpet for the floor, and because he used it when he was travelling for interviews with personages of every grade of importance, it could be divided into a Sitting-room and a bedroom.

In the least time possible, Hawkins had a table set for dinner.

There was hot water for Lord Athelstan to wash, and a bottle of wine, which had quite unnecessarily been further cooled in a clump of snow, was opened.

He changed as a matter of course from the clothes he had worn all day.

It was part of the self-discipline that he expected not only of himself but of every civilised person with whom he came into contact, that they should wash and change before dinner.

He came from his bedroom into the Sitting-room.

There were two servants to wait on him, supervised by Hawkins. They too were wearing clean clothes.

It was not a long dinner, but it was an excellent one, and when it was finished, Lord Athelstan lit a cigar.

Sitting back in the collapsible chair that was carried by one of the pack-horses, he accepted a glass of brandy and felt at peace with the world.

The servants withdrew to have their own supper and Lord Athelstan sat thinking of what a strange journey it had been, and how Shamyl had exceeded his expectations in being even more magnetic a personality than he had anticipated.

"He is a great man," he told himself.

Then as he extinguished his cigar, he thought the sooner he went to bed the earlier he could rise and be on his way to Tiflis.

He finished his brandy. Then as he set down the glass there was a sudden cry.

"Wolves, M'Lord! Wolves!"

It was Hawkins' voice sounding the alarm.

Lord Athelstan flung on his fur-lined cloak and reached for his pistols.

Chapter Three

It was cold outside, but not the biting ice-cold of Daghestan.

It was dark but there was a faint light from the stars which cast a luminous glow on the white snows above them.

As Lord Athelstan reached the little knot of his men who had already taken up their positions facing towards the mountains, he could see, as his eyes grew accustomed to the darkness, moving shadows.

They were circling beyond the lights of the camp and he knew they were the wolves.

He had picked up, as he left his tent, two pepper-box pistols, muzzle-loading, each with six barrels.

They were the very latest weapons which he had brought with him from England, and he knew that Hawkins also had a pair. The other men were not so well provided and would have to re-load their guns after each shot.

At this time of the year, when the wolves

had grown thin and increasingly savage during the privation of the winter months, it was inevitable that they should come down into the valley at night.

They stole as food the lambs, the goat-kids and every other young animal which could not escape from them.

The farmers suffered severe losses, but however many wolves they destroyed, nothing could ever rid the Caucasus mountains of the packs of ravenous beasts.

"How many are there?" Lord Athelstan asked one of his men.

Always when they encamped there was a sentry on duty, for fear not only of wolves, but also of thieves and tribes who looked on travellers as their natural prey.

"I do not think it is a big pack, M'Lord," the man replied.

They were all silent watching the animals moving in front of them, being at times indistinguishable from the rocks or shrubs, and at other times clearly evident by the glint of their eyes and a flash of their bared teeth.

Lord Athelstan knew they would reconnoitre for some time and then, if their leader was courageous, they would rush the camp.

He had an instinct that this was about to

happen and his hands tightened on the barrels of his pistols waiting tensely.

Suddenly they came.

There were more of them than he had expected, their leader springing forward snarling, his teeth and eyes grotesque in the flames from the fire around which the tents had been erected.

Lord Athelstan fired first and his men followed him.

His pistol accounted for the leading wolf and for three others, but still they came.

The noise of the firing was deafening and Lord Athelstan saw with something like consternation that his men were not as accurate as he had hoped, or else the wolves were tough enough to continue advancing even with bullets in their bodies.

The men reloaded and fired again and Lord Athelstan realised that he had expended all six barrels in one pistol and only had a few shots left in the other.

He started to re-load and as he did so was aware that Hawkins was firing on his left side and that the man on his right also had a pepper-box pistol.

He knew that Hawkins must have shared his weapons and was surprised.

It was unlike him to be so generous. He was inordinately proud of having been entrusted to handle a pistol similar to his master's.

The wolves were hesitating; their advance had been checked but they were still hungry enough to make another attempt.

Then as Lord Athelstan, his pistols reloaded, was waiting to fire again, the wolves obviously more hungry than cautious, fell on the dead bodies of their companions and started to tear them apart.

It was only a few seconds before the rest of the pack followed their example.

It was then easy to shoot them as they quarrelled, snarled and fought amongst themselves, pulling the carcasses in pieces and oblivious of any other danger.

Lord Athelstan shot them down one after another. Finally only half a dozen escaped all dragging with them a part of their mauled and mangled companions.

He fired the remaining bullets in his pistols after them but it was difficult in the darkness to know whether he had scored a hit.

He looked around at his men.

"Well done!" he said. "Pull what is left of the dead wolves out of reach. Those who escaped may return for them."

The men hurried to obey and Lord Athelstan turned to speak to the man who had stood on his right firing one of Hawkins' pepper-box pistols. But he was not there.

Reloading his weapons as he went, Lord Athelstan walked back to his own tent.

Hawkins followed him to take his fur-lined cloak from his shoulders and put it down where it had been before, just inside the opening of the tent.

"I might have anticipated that we should have visitors of that sort tonight," Lord Athelstan said in genial tones. "Commend the man who was on sentry duty and saw them first."

"I will, M'Lord!"

"And by the way, who was the man to whom you loaned one of your pepper-box pistols? I have never known you do that before. He was a good shot!"

There was a moment's silence and then Hawkins answered:

"As he is Your Lordship's guest I thought it was only right, M'Lord."

"My guest?" Lord Athelstan exclaimed.

"Yes, M'Lord. It was the Indian gentleman. The Naib informed me that he was travelling with us as far as Constantinople."

Lord Athelstan was suddenly still. Then in a voice unexpectedly sharp he said:

"Show him in here!"

"Yes, M'Lord."

Lord Athelstan was aware that Hawkins was surprised at the tone in which he had spoken but he had suddenly a terrible suspicion of who the stranger might be.

He could hardly believe it possible, and yet where Shamyl was concerned would he have expected him not to be determined to get his own way?

Some minutes passed. Then Hawkins drew back the flap of the tent.

"His Highness, Prince Akbar of Sharpura, M'Lord!"

The visitor came into the tent and Hawkins removed his goatskin *bourkha* to lay it beside His Lordship's own cloak. Then he retired securing the flap against the night air.

Natasha Melikov stood looking at Lord Athelstan and for a moment neither of them said anything.

She was dressed in the long tight-waisted, high-necked brocade coat of a Rajput Prince.

She wore a blue turban and Lord Athelstan saw that she had darkened the skin of her face and hands.

Her eyes were faintly outlined with kohl and beneath the brocade coat her legs were encased around the ankles in the white tightly-wound trouser-like garment which was worn by the Northern tribes.

Angry though he was, Lord Athelstan could not help acknowledging that her disguise was extremely effective.

She did in fact look very much like a young Indian Prince, and there was something in the pride and dignity with which she faced him which made the illusion even more convincing.

At last he found his voice.

"How dare you!" he exclaimed. "How dare you inflict yourself on me when I made it very clear both to you and the Imam that I would not escort you!"

"There was no other way I could save my brother," Natasha answered.

"That is your problem and not mine!" Lord Athelstan snapped. "You will return to Dargo-Vedin. I will have no part in this!"

"Do you expect me to leave tonight or are you prepared to send me to-morrow?" Natasha enquired. "I shall require an escort of four men."

Lord Athelstan's lips tightened with fury.

He could not at the moment spare four men or their horses unless he was to sacrifice a large amount of his personal equipment.

There were others of his staff who were to meet him in Tiflis.

He had sent them there direct from the

Persian border with the bulk of his baggage which there had been no point in taking on the perilous ride to Dargo-Vedin.

But he had no desire to take Natasha with him to Tiflis, and anyway if his men arrived with four of their number missing it was quite obvious they would gossip amongst themselves.

Lord Athelstan was well aware that a whisper in the Bazaars of Tiflis would be known in the Viceroy's Salon before evening.

Was he prepared to explain, he asked himself, the reasons why, having brought one of the imprisoned Princesses as far as the Georgian valley, he had deliberately sent her back into captivity?

He realised the *impasse* in which he found himself and this made him angrier than ever; but because he always had an iron self-control he did not rage at the woman facing him, but his voice was icy and like a whiplash as he said:

"I am appalled and disgusted by your presumption! I did not believe Shamyl would treat me so treacherously. I shall certainly not further his cause with Britain!"

"To penalise Shamyl would be unjust and spiteful!" Natasha retorted. "You have every reason, My Lord, to be incensed, but

81

because you have been out-witted I did not expect you to be unsporting and petty about it!"

"You have used some very hard words to me, Countess, ever since we met," Lord Athelstan replied, "but you can hardly expect me to be pleased to jeopardise my career for an action on your part of which I utterly disapprove and which in fact disgusts me!"

"It need not disgust you any more than the thought of my being raped by a barbarous Tartar in a crumbling aôul," Natasha retorted.

She sat down in one of the chairs at the table. As she did so he realised that she was as angry as he was. Yet she too was self-controlled and only the flashing of her dark eyes told him of the resentment burning within her.

"Can we talk of this sensibly, My Lord?" she asked.

"There is nothing sensible about it!" Lord Athelstan replied, "but I am prepared to listen to what you have to say to me."

"That is indeed generous of Your Lordship!" Natasha replied sarcastically, "since you have no alternative."

"I could throw you to the wolves!" he said.

There was a twist of amusement at the corners of her mouth.

"That would be very un-English," she answered, "but doubtless it would be a compensation to listen to the crunching of my bones!"

She paused to add:

"They would still be hungry. There is very little flesh left on my body after living in the Imam's house."

She was trying to shame him, Lord Athelstan knew. At the same time he could not help being vividly aware of how thin she was from her imprisonment.

It struck him too how stiff and tired she must be after the last two days' gruelling ride, when she had been unable to take exercise for so many months.

Princess Anna had told him how confined they had been in Shamyl's hands.

"May I offer you a glass of wine?" he asked.

She looked at him and now there was laughter in her eyes.

"Beware of the Greeks when they come bearing gifts!" she quoted. "Are you trying to persuade me to go back voluntarily?"

"Actually I was thinking you must be tired," Lord Athelstan replied.

"I am!" she answered. "At the same time I

would not trust you not to trick me!"

"As you have tricked me!" he answered. "I assure you, Countess, I would do so without hesitation, if I could think of how it was possible."

Lord Athelstan brought the bottle of brandy from which he had been drinking earlier in the evening from the leather wine-box embossed with a coronet in which his drink was carried on a pack-horse.

He placed it on the table, produced two glasses and half-filled them.

"Let us drink without prejudice to what we have to say to each other."

As Natasha lifted the brandy to her lips, he saw her thin fingers were trembling and knew she was in fact very tired.

Quite suddenly it struck him how brave she was, and yet he told himself that he must not weaken in his conviction that he must be rid of her.

As if she read his thoughts she took another sip of the brandy and asked:

"Well, have you decided to murder me or send me back in chains?"

"You know full well I can do neither," Lord Athelstan replied, and now once again he was extremely angry.

He could not arrive at Tiflis with a woman disguised as a man, and not even an ordinary woman, but a prisoner of the Imam.

A woman who was prepared to sacrifice herself in an exaggerated and ridiculous manner which once it was known, would cause an immense sensation over the whole of the Christian world.

"Listen to me," he said forcefully. "You cannot do this thing! I know you love your brother and that you wish to save him, but the way you are trying to do so is impossible!"

"Why?" Natasha enquired.

"You know the reasons as well as I do," Lord Athelstan replied in an irritated tone. "What you do not understand is that it is only a question of time before Shamyl is defeated. He cannot hold out much longer against the Russians. His army is depleted. They are being driven further and further back from the territories they once held and Field-Marshal Bariatinsky is harassing them all the time."

"If the Russians do reach Dargo-Vedin," Natasha replied, "do you imagine there will be many left alive to tell the tale? You know as well as I do that the Caucasians die fighting."

This was indisputable and Lord Athelstan could not contradict it.

The Caucasian warriors always preferred

death to being disarmed. The mystique of the sword for Shamyl's Murids was not understood by the Russians for a long time.

"I have the chance to save my brother," Natasha went on, "but the only choice as far as I am concerned is between a Naib or a Sultan."

She shrugged her shoulders expressively.

"I cannot see that one is any worse or more unpleasant than the other."

She gave a deep sigh and added:

"Dimitri will go home. That is all that matters."

"I suppose you expect me to admire what you are doing," Lord Athelstan asked bitterly.

"I expect nothing from you, My Lord," Natasha replied, "except what I can extort by blackmail or treachery."

She drank down the rest of her brandy and it seemed to give her a fresh impetus to say:

"You will take me with you because you have no alternative. No-one will guess who I am. To your servants, to everyone we meet, I am a Rajput Prince, the son of the Maharajah of Sharpura. You brought me with you from India. Who is going to question such a story?"

Lord Athelstan pressed his lips together

to prevent himself raging at her.

Her sheer audacity and impertinence seemed to him intolerable and yet he did not know how to reply.

It was true it would be quite unexceptional for him to allow a young Prince who wished to visit Britain to travel with him.

If there was in fact a Maharajah of Sharpura and he had asked him for such a service, he would have acquiesced even though he thought it a nuisance.

Yet to arrive at Tiflis with one of Shamyl's prisoners, about whom the whole of Russia was concerned, and not to hand her over to the care of her own people was an act so incredible, so unprecedented that Lord Athelstan could find no words in which to express his distaste of the whole plot.

"Damn you!" he said forcibly. "This is not a moment for playing charades; for hoping that you will not be recognised or discovered. If you have to behave in such a ridiculous manner, why should I be a part of it?"

"I accused you of being a coward when we first met," Natasha replied. "Now I will add to it the charge of being grossly selfish. You are, My Lord, thinking only of yourself."

"I am thinking of my position as representative of Her Britannic Majesty Queen Victoria," Lord Athelstan retorted.

"All very impressive!" Natasha mocked, "and I am sure you look very pretty in your diplomat's uniform. But I am concerned with saving my brother's life and I do not care what I do."

"That is obvious!"

"Just trust me," Natasha begged. "I promise you that I will not let you down! You will not be discovered with a woman in your baggage, if that is what worries you! Besides, if they did, it is doubtful if anyone in Tiflis would be shocked."

"That obviously depends on the woman," Lord Athelstan said.

"That is true, but no-one will point a finger of scorn at your kindness in escorting a young Indian on his first visit to this country. And I promise you I am a very good actress!"

"All women are born deceivers!" Lord Athelstan said bitterly.

"Has that been your experience?" Natasha asked. "Who broke your heart?"

There was an audacity in the question which brought a frown to Lord Athelstan's brow.

"I think, Countess," he said coldly, "if we are to take part in these amateur theatricals it would be wisest for us to avoid personalities."

"Meaning you are longing to say some very unpleasant things to me," Natasha replied. "Well say them! I assure you I am far more thick-skinned than you are!"

"That I can well believe!" Lord Athelstan snapped.

She gave a little laugh of sheer amusement.

"You are a bad loser, My Lord. At the same time I perceive that you have already acknowledged defeat. We act what you call 'this charade' together!"

"Without my approval, against every decent instinct in my body, and with a feeling of frustration and fury in my heart," Lord Athelstan said violently.

Natasha's eyes opened wide.

"So you have a heart?" she exclaimed. "I was beginning to doubt it!"

Lord Athelstan rose from his chair.

He was so angry that he felt at that moment an insane desire to take Natasha by the shoulders and shake her.

It was something he had never felt before about a woman, and he knew that in some extraordinary manner this young Russian girl had got under his skin.

Every word she said was an irritation.

It was not only her audacity in forcing herself upon him after he had already refused to do what she asked.

That was bad enough.

But now deliberately to provoke him, to jeer and jibe at him in a manner which he had never experienced before, was to arouse feelings that no other woman had ever been able to.

"It is quite obvious to me," he said, "that not even imprisonment or starvation has managed to produce in you the feminine graces which all women worthy of the name should have."

He thought Natasha looked amused and went on:

"Spoilt, cosseted and adulated all your life, you think that you can get your own way and do what you like simply because you are an aristocrat. Well, let me tell you, Countess, I dislike you just as I dislike your behaviour and it is intolerable for me to think that I must submit to being in your presence as far as Constantinople!"

"Plain speaking, My Lord!" Natasha retorted.

"And I shall continue to speak plainly," Lord Athelstan replied. "I have never before met a woman who was supposed to be a gentlewoman who could behave in such an outrageous manner."

"Then it will be a good experience for

you!" Natasha said. "Think how amusingly it will read in your memoirs!"

"I think, Countess," Lord Athelstan said slowly, "you had best retire to bed. If you stay here I may say or even do something I would afterwards regret!"

"You would like to strike me, would you not?" Natasha enquired. "It is only your English upbringing and your public school principles which prevent you from doing so."

"I can only hope that one day," Lord Athelstan said bitterly, "you marry a man who takes a whip to you!"

"As Russian peasants do to their wives," Natasha smiled. "It is a stimulating thought and certainly an idea to sleep on!"

She rose to her feet.

"Good-night, My Lord. I cannot tell you how much I am looking forward to our journey together and to an association which I feel quite sure will be very instructive."

She spoke sarcastically. Then mockingly she put her hands together, palm to palm, finger to finger, in the traditional Indian greeting.

"Salaam, Sahib!"

Before Lord Athelstan could think of a suitable reply she had picked up her *bourkha* and was gone from the tent.

He stood where she had left him, his hands clenched together in an effort at self-control, knowing he was angrier than he had ever been before in his life, seething with a fury because he was so frustrated.

This woman could defy and taunt him; could ignore what he said; could thrust herself upon him with the collusion of the Imam; and there was nothing he could do about it!

It was not only that she was laughing at him.

He was well aware that Shamyl would feel he had scored with truly Oriental subtlety over the slower-thinking, unintuitive Englishman.

"Damn him! Damn them all!" Lord Athelstan exclaimed.

Then he was astonished with himself for being shaken out of his habitual reserve, the cool calmness for which he was notorious, and the control on which he prided himself.

"What does it matter?" he asked and knew that it mattered more than he dared to admit.

Lord Athelstan passed a restless night and when he came from his sleeping-tent to find that Natasha was already seated at the breakfast-table it did not appease his feeling of irritation.

The morning, warm and windless, was brilliant with sunshine.

Hawkins had drawn away the sides of the tent from the part which was constructed as a Sitting-room and Lord Athelstan could look over the green valley in which they were encamped.

There was blossom on the fruit trees, flowers were blooming profusely in the grass, and he knew that the Winter had been left behind in Daghestan.

At his entrance Natasha rose from the chair in which she had been sitting.

"Good-morning, My Lord!" she said politely and almost humbly.

But she said it with an Indian intonation and Lord Athelstan realised she was giving a performance in front of Hawkins and the other servants who were waiting on them.

"Good-morning!" Lord Athelstan replied sharply, then reluctantly he added: "Your Highness!"

'If we have to play this blasted game,' he thought to himself, 'I had better do it convincingly.'

Hawkins, he knew, would be hard to deceive, whatever the other servants might think or not think.

He also wondered apprehensively whether a woman would be taken in by Natasha's appearance.

Then he told himself that if he regarded her critically, without prejudice, it would be very difficult to guess that she was not in fact a young man.

She was so thin that there were certainly no soft feminine curves beneath the straight, tight coat, and Rajput Princes were noted for the beauty of their faces and their exquisite features.

Natasha's nose was too short, but many of the Northern Tribes did not have the high-bridged nose so prevalent in Rajput por-traits, and their skin was lighter than that of the Indians from the South.

Apart from these details known to Lord Athelstan because he had travelled in India, it was unlikely there would be many people in Tiflis who had known any Indians, let alone visited their country.

Despite his worries, Lord Athelstan ate a substantial breakfast, although he noticed that Natasha ate very little and guessed it was because after months of deprivation she was finding it difficult to absorb food.

As soon as he had finished Lord Athelstan rose to his feet.

"We must leave!" he said abruptly.

He was just about to go outside and mount the stallion that was waiting for him, when one of his men came to the side of the tent and spoke to Hawkins.

Lord Athelstan waited.

"There are some soldiers approaching, M'Lord."

Almost before Hawkins said the words there was the sound of horses being brought to a standstill.

A moment later an officer in Russian uniform came towards the tent, his epaulettes and decorations glinting in the sun.

Lord Athelstan walked forward to meet him.

The Officer saluted smartly.

"You are Lord Athelstan?" he asked in quite passable English.

"I am!"

"I have a message for you, M'Lord, from Colonel Prince David Tchavtchavadze. He is at Vladikavkaz and he asks if Your Lordship would do him the honour of meeting him as soon as possible."

Lord Athelstan was not surprised at the invitation.

He was certain that Prince David would be somewhere in the vicinity awaiting with Djemmal Eddin the results of the negotiations for the exchange of the hostages.

"Please inform Prince David," Lord Athelstan said to the Officer, "that I will come to Vladikavkaz immediately."

"We are here to escort you, My Lord. My name is Gagarin — Captain Ivan Gagarin."

"I am delighted to meet you, Captain," Lord Athelstan said holding out his hand.

As he did so he was aware that Natasha had risen from the table. She joined him at the entrance to the tent.

He knew it was a deliberate action on her part and now there was nothing he could do but say with what grace he could muster:

"Your Highness, allow me to present Captain Gagarin — Prince Akbar of Sharpura."

He was aware as he spoke that the Captain was surprised, and he was forced to explain.

"His Highness has travelled with me from India. He is journeying to England for the first time."

Even as he spoke he knew it was a triumph for Natasha. She had won!

She had forced him into a position where he had to acknowledge her, and now that he had taken the first step there could be no retreat.

He could not be rid of her, and he was obliged, however much it infuriated him, to take part in a deception which, if it were exposed, would ruin his career and cause a sensation which would be attached to him for the rest of his life.

"The Prince's invitation is of course extended to Your Highness," the Captain said to Natasha.

"I am very grateful," Natasha answered.

They set off a few minutes later leaving Lord Athelstan's servants to strike camp and follow them more slowly.

Vladikavkaz was a typical garrison town and a trading-post between Russia, the Caucasus and the Trans-Caucasian provinces.

There were the usual bazaars in which travellers and soldiers, when they had any money, could purchase fine rugs, silver and ivory, Persian silks, saddles and spices.

But the most popular articles were daggers and other weapons inlaid with silver and ivory.

Owing to the prosperity which had been brought to Vladikavkaz through its being a military base, there were Persian and Russian steam-baths, Clubs, shops, Restaurants and some quite impressive-looking private houses.

Towering above the town was the Governor's House, and it was here that Lord

Athelstan learnt that Prince David was staying at the moment, and, with him, Djemmal Eddin.

They had been together, he gathered from Captain Gagarin, ever since he had arrived at Vladikavkaz at the beginning of February.

He shared quarters with Prince David, and because of the sacrifice he was to make in giving up what had become to him his whole life in exchange for the freedom of the captured Princesses, the Russians could not do enough for him.

Both his brother officers and the inhabitants of all the garrison towns between Tiflis and Vladikavkaz gave balls and suppers, receptions and parties in his honour.

"What does Djemmal Eddin feel about returning to his own country?" Lord Athelstan asked Captain Gagarin as they rode over the beautiful green country-side.

"I think the question is," Captain Gagarin answered, "which country now is his own?"

This Lord Athelstan felt was a very pertinent query when he met Djemmal Eddin.

The young man looked very much the same as when he had last seen him in St. Petersburg, just as charming, just as attractive, except his large dark eyes were even more mournful than Lord Athelstan remembered them.

Now there was something almost agonising about the expression on his face, as if he knew that what awaited him was not only the annihilation but the crucifixion of all he held dear.

When Lord Athelstan had related to Prince David everything Princess Anna had said to him in the brief conversation he had with her at Dargo-Vedin, it was inevitable they should speak of Djemmal Eddin.

He was not in the room and Prince David said: "I have never met a Moslem with so little of the Tartar about him."

He gave a sigh.

"The boy is Russian and completely Europeanised."

"I can see that!" Lord Athelstan answered.

"What I admire about him," the Prince went on, "is that he refuses to be lionised or pitied. He will not assume the romantic character of the deliverer."

But Lord Athelstan realised that was how he appeared to everyone.

He could not help wondering as he talked with the Prince, with Natasha sitting beside him, what she thought and felt.

She would see how deeply moved everyone in Vladikavkaz was at the price

Djemmal Eddin must pay for the release of the hostages.

If he had not been so angry he would have been amused to realise how easily Natasha was accepted as an Indian. Her appearance caused little comment simply because the Russians were concentrating on Djemmal Eddin.

There was, however, an acute feeling of tension which was inescapable.

Negotiations between Shamyl and the Russians for the exchange of hostages were still not finalised.

"The difficulty is," Prince David said to Lord Athelstan, "I cannot find any more money. It is impossible for me to raise more than the 40,000 roubles I have offered them already."

He made a sound of frustrated anger as he went on:

"They keep suggesting I should write to the Tzar and the Government, but how can I ask them to pay the ransom for private individuals and swell the Murid coffers?"

"I quite understand it would be impossible," Lord Athelstan agreed.

He told Prince David how he was certain that it was not Shamyl who was the stumbling-block, but the rapacity of the Murids.

"For the first time," Lord Athelstan explained, "they have realised their power."

"Blasted barbarians!" Prince David ejaculated.

It was hard to know what words to find to comfort the man who was tortured by the thought of his wife and family in the hands of his enemies.

What was more, the letters Princess Anna wrote to her husband were growing, Lord Athelstan gathered, more and more depressed as it seemed there would be no end to their suffering.

"We must not detain you too long here at Vladikavkaz," Prince David said to Lord Athelstan, "and we are in fact accompanying you to Tiflis where the Viceroy is expecting you."

He forced a smile to his lips as he added:

"Yet another Ball is being given for Djemmal Eddin. I think we are growing a little tired of them, but for him they are his 'swan-song'. He knows that once he leaves Georgia he will never waltz again."

"Are you quite sure the Viceroy is expecting me?" Lord Athelstan asked. "I thought perhaps it would be best if I pressed on towards Constantinople."

He knew as he spoke that he had previously arranged to meet Prince Voronzov.

At the same time he was nervous of staying at the Palace because Natasha was with him.

"I assure you," Prince David replied, "His Excellency is looking forward eagerly to your visit. I have also sent a message back to tell him that Prince Akbar is with you."

There was nothing Lord Athelstan could do in the circumstances but express his gratitude. But before they left Vladikavkaz he had the opportunity of a private conversation with Natasha.

"Perhaps it would be better," he said, "if I send you ahead so that you do not have to stay in Tiflis. We could meet at Batoum."

"Still afraid?" Natasha asked mockingly.

"Of course I am afraid of discovery!" Lord Athelstan answered almost roughly. "You see what the feeling is here. People think and talk of nothing but the exchange of hostages. What do you imagine would happen if they knew that I had with me a hostage and was deliberately conveying her to another prison?"

"Disclosure would certainly be dramatic!" Natasha said lightly. "We must just be careful not to betray ourselves!"

"Ourselves!" Lord Athelstan groaned. "How I ever became involved in this appalling deception I shall never know!"

"Perhaps it was fate!" Natasha said sweetly. "Fate that you should be instructed to visit Shamyl, fate that I should be waiting for you there!"

"It was certainly my most unfortunate day when I encountered you," Lord Athelstan said.

"Your gallantry overwhelms me!" she replied. "Stop trembling. Anyone who is clairvoyant would know only too well you were hiding something."

"You are certainly the skeleton in the cupboard!" Lord Athelstan retorted.

She laughed.

"There you certainly score a point! Up to now I have undoubtedly been the victor!"

Once again Lord Athelstan had an irrepressible desire to shake her; but because he was determined not to give her the satisfaction of realising how greatly she annoyed him he walked away, conscious as he did so that she was still laughing.

They reached Tiflis late in the afternoon.

The Georgian capital looked at its best with its spires, towers and roofs glinting gold in the sunshine.

The trees surrounding it were heavy with blossom, the river as they passed over the bridge built by Alexander the Great moved like molten silver between its steep banks.

Prince David and Djemmal Eddin were staying in Military Headquarters, but they escorted Lord Athelstan and Natasha to the Viceroy's Palace.

It was a magnificent setting for Prince Voronzov's traditional pomp and the appropriate background for his tall, dignified figure which had been so much a part of the historic Caucasian battles.

Now, at seventy-three, he was growing old, but he still had a presence which made him a distinctive, rather awe-inspiring personality who could never be ignored.

The marble colonnades of the Palace, its gigantic chandeliers and gilded furniture, were a magnificent and an almost unbelievable contrast, where Djemmal Eddin was concerned, to the Great Aôul.

They dined off gold-plate at dinner, waited on by lackeys in the crimson and white Voronzov livery. There were three hundred of them in the Palace.

The dinner consisted of twenty courses and Lord Athelstan wondered how much Natasha would be able to consume.

The Princess Eliza Voronzov, who wore a necklace of huge turquoises and diamonds, employed as a page a dwarf with huge moustachios. He wore a fantastic uniform.

This was in accordance with the Russian

love of spectacular servants. The Empress was always followed by her negro pages, who wore enormous baggy trousers and plumed turbans.

Lord Athelstan watched the ladies flirting and doing everything they could to attract the unhappy Djemmal Eddin. He wondered how it would be possible to make the Murids realise that Prince David could not in fact raise the million roubles they required as a ransom.

Lord Athelstan was quite sure that every detail of this dinner and every other reception given in his son's honour was related to Shamyl.

Later in the evening during the Ball he watched Djemmal Eddin waltzing with the local beauties.

The candlelight shimmered on the decorations of the officers and on the jewels encircling the white necks of the ladies whose crinolines, just introduced from Paris, swung around to the strains of a string-orchestra.

Lord Athelstan then walked through an open window onto the terrace outside.

The garden was filled with oleander bushes in bloom, and acacia and eucalyptus trees cast dark shadows.

Because he knew the East so well Lord

Athelstan was certain that Shamyl's spies were watching everything that happened.

The Imam would not only wish to know what his son was doing. He would also want to be quite certain that it was really Djemmal Eddin who was to be exchanged for the captured Princesses.

Knowing the austerity of the Imam's life Lord Athelstan thought the reports from his spies would be disturbing, to say the least of it.

For a Moslem to be dancing, embracing what to them were half-naked Christian women, drinking wine and smoking cigars, was to be lost to Allah.

As he was thinking these things Lord Athelstan heard a light step behind him on the terrace and was aware before he saw her that Natasha had joined him.

"Are you thinking of Djemmal Eddin?" she asked.

"I was," he admitted.

"I have been thinking of him too," Natasha answered, "and of myself."

"Why do you not change your mind?" Lord Athelstan asked. "Appear as a woman and tell your people you have escaped from captivity."

"Would you do that in similar circumstances?" she asked in a low voice.

"I am a man," he answered.

"You have already told me I am un-feminine."

"I still think it would be the sensible thing to do."

"And leave my brother in the hell to which Djemmal Eddin is going?"

There was no answer to this.

With an irritated gesture Lord Athelstan threw his cigar away over the balcony of the terrace on which they stood.

It fell onto the ground below and he heard the hiss as it extinguished itself in the damp grass.

"The fact that you are here will be reported to Shamyl," he said. "Make quite certain of that!"

"You mean . . . there are . . . eyes watching . . . us?"

"Not only you, but Djemmal Eddin."

"I might have known that," she said. "All the time we were in the Great Aôul there was always someone listening to what we said. I think such lack of privacy is terrifying!"

"It is part of the East," Lord Athelstan remarked.

"And of Russia!"

Natasha paused for a moment and then in a low voice as if she spoke to herself she went on:

"That is why I would like to go to England. I wish I really were Prince Akbar! I have always dreamt of the Freedom of England; of not being afraid of what I have to say; of not having to look over my shoulder."

Lord Athelstan did not reply and she gave a little sigh.

"It is no use setting our sights too high," she said bravely. "As Your Lordship well knows, Constantinople is my goal."

She turned away from him as she spoke and walked back into the Ball-room.

He had a feeling that at that moment she wanted to look at the dancing, to observe the grandeur, the elegance and the beauty of those who waltzed.

Like Djemmal Eddin, for her also it would be the last time!

Chapter Four

Lord Athelstan walked into the Sitting-room which was part of the Suite he and Natasha had been given in the Viceroy's Palace.

As he handed his hat and gloves to a servant he saw that Natasha was waiting for him.

She had risen to her feet at his entrance and her dark eyes were on his as he advanced across the Aubusson carpet and under a huge crystal chandelier which decorated the centre of the ornate room.

She waited until the door had shut behind the servant, then she said:

"Is everything all right?"

Lord Athelstan saw the anxiety in her face and realised that for once she was not defying or taunting him but was in fact very anxious.

"Come and sit down," he said, "and I will tell you what occurred."

He had risen very early in the morning to

ride with Prince David, Djemmal Eddin and a number of other officers to Hassif Yourt where they were to meet the messengers from the Imam.

As they travelled Lord Athelstan had learnt that the Prince David was desperately depressed, having that morning received a letter from his wife.

He told Lord Athelstan that Princess Anna had written:

Today they were going to distribute us amongst the Naibs. We thought we were lost, but his sons asked Shamyl to send messengers to you for the last time.

"I cannot believe that is true," Lord Athelstan had said. "I can only imagine that the Imam is frightening Princess Anna so that she will write to you in such a vein."

"My wife goes on," Prince David replied with a break in his voice:

It seems as if it is not God's will that we should see each other again in this world!

"What can I reply to that?"

"I am absolutely convinced," Lord

Athelstan answered, "that however many threats they make, Shamyl is determined to have his son back with him. After all, he has waited thirteen years for this moment."

"I cannot find a million roubles," Prince David said desperately.

"I do not believe that money counts with Shamyl," Lord Athelstan said. "I have seen the austerity in which he lives. I have been in his house which has practically no comforts in it whatsoever."

"This avarice comes from the Murids, who apparently now rule their Leader," Prince David said bitterly.

"That is what they wish us to believe," Lord Athelstan replied. "Personally I think that Shamyl is far too astute to lose the chance of having his son back in his arms by allowing himself to be overruled by his own followers."

"I wish I could believe you," Prince David said. "We will see what transpires this morning."

They reached Hassif Yourt which was a garrison town and nearest to the place Shamyl had chosen for the exchange of hostages.

This was a flat plateau on the edge of his own territory, the Greater Tchetchnia. It sloped down to the water so that his troops would have the shelter of the wooded hills.

Across the River Mitchik the Georgian country was open and unwooded and could therefore easily be raked by gunfire if at the last moment the exchange should become a battle.

In the meantime it seemed as if the Imam's negotiators were determined to make difficulties.

Lord Athelstan was well aware he had been invited by Prince David to accompany him and Djemmal Eddin to this morning's meeting so that he could see and report to Great Britain the manner in which Shamyl was prevaricating, temporising and putting obstacles in the way of what would normally have been a simple exchange of hostages.

This was very evident when finally they arrived at Hassif Yourt to find that the Imam had written a letter to Prince David.

The Prince, after he had read it, showed the letter to Lord Athelstan.

One sentence in it summed up all the difficulties:

You must know that besides my son I require a million roubles and 150 of my Murids whom you hold prisoner. Do not bargain with me, I will take no less. If you do not comply, I have resolved to distribute your family among the different aôuls.

It was obvious that the Prince was thunderstruck.

For the moment he was silent and then in a voice hoarse with rage he said to the Messengers:

"I will make no further reply to your Imam. You can tell him from me that long ago I took an eternal farewell of my family. I can only trust them now to God's mercy."

He drew a deep breath.

"If by Saturday you do not bring back to me here the solemn acceptance of my original offer, I swear by the Creator that on that day I will leave Hassif Yourt and take Djemmal Eddin away with me."

He went on, his voice gathering fury, to say that from the day Shamyl carried out his threat of sending his wife and children to the aôuls he would no longer recognise them and would never in the future receive them back.

When the Prince had finished speaking everyone was silent, too abashed by his violence to reply. Then at length the Messengers who had listened with stony faces asked if he would put this ultimatum to the Imam in writing.

"I will not write another line," the Prince replied harshly. "I am sorry to have wasted so much paper on a man who consistently breaks his word."

The Murids began to answer, but the Prince turned from them in disgust and made as if to leave the room.

"There is one other way," their leader said after a moment. "The Imam would agree to let your family go in exchange for his son and only 40,000 roubles but in that case Princess Varvara and her child must remain with him. Her release would then be a matter for later negotiations."

Prince David now lost all control of his temper.

He would have struck the Messengers had not Djemmal Eddin and some of the other officers present restrained him.

"Not only will I not leave my sister-in-law with you," shouted the Prince, "but I will not even allow the youngest of my servants' children to be detained."

In the uproar which ensued everyone talked at once, and Lord Athelstan noticed that Djemmal Eddin had turned crimson with rage and humiliation at the way in which his people were behaving.

For one moment Lord Athelstan thought he might have drawn his pistol on them, but finally the Officers managed to calm both Prince David and Djemmal Eddin and the Messengers were hurried from the room.

The Russians decided to send to Shamyl an Armenian interpreter who had been present on all the previous negotiations.

He was serving with the Russian Army and was an extremely astute and diplomatic man.

"I am sure," Lord Athelstan said as he finished telling Natasha what had occurred, "Shamyl will not want to lose his son at the eleventh hour. The Caucasian tie of blood is sacred, and Shamyl will, I am convinced, find a way to accept the Prince's offer which will save everyone's face."

"The whole situation is intolerable!" Natasha said hotly.

"There is always a lot of sabre-rattling which comes to nothing," Lord Athelstan said soothingly. "I am sure that in the end Princess Anna will be returned and with her all the Prince's household."

"Except Dimitri," Natasha said in a low voice. "I know Shamyl will never let him go. I could see in his eyes when he talked to me that he had the idea of bringing up Dimitri as a Caucasian, just as the Tzar had made Djemmal Eddin a Russian."

There was a pain in her voice that Lord

Athelstan had never heard before.

As he wondered how he could comfort her she said in an entirely different tone:

"Will you give me some money?"

He started and then replied:

"Of course. How remiss of me! I should have thought of it before, but seeing how you were dressed . . ."

He looked as he spoke at the rich material of her princely coat and the exquisite silk of the pink turban she wore on her head.

There was a faint smile on Natasha's lips as she explained:

"The mountain nobles raid the merchants' caravans as they file through the passes. They make off with silks and brocades and fine furs from Tiflis and the East, carried by the camels northwards."

She made a little gesture with her hands before she went on:

"They also intercept the baggage trains coming south to Tiflis laden with goods from Moscow and St. Petersburg — French laces, ribbons, cloth, gold watches and china."

"I am surprised that Shamyl should stoop to thieving!" Lord Athelstan remarked.

"He does not do it himself," Natasha replied, "but he accepts presents from his nobles as in other countries a Leader might impose taxes. He also makes quite sure that he has his fair share of the booty of war."

She looked down at her brocade coat.

"This, like the other things I wear, came from a sort of Aladdin's cave in the Great Aôul."

"I should imagine it came originally from Persia," Lord Athelstan said.

"Or even from India," Natasha answered. "The Imam has so much stored away, gold dishes, jewel-studded sabre-scabbards, coral and amber drinking cups, that I realised it was a reserve for the future."

She gave a sigh.

"To be sold to pay for guns, pistols and swords. A Caucasian cannot live without killing!"

There was a sharp bitterness in her voice. Then she smiled.

"I was allowed to take what was necessary but not of course a *kindjal,* which is what I need now, or even a sharper dagger."

Lord Athelstan looked at her enquiringly and with that defiant air that he knew so well she said:

"You should be pleased to give me money for a weapon with which I can kill myself!"

Lord Athelstan who had drawn a well-filled wallet from an inside pocket of his coat, stiffened.

"Must you talk in that abominable manner?" he asked.

"Why abominable?" Natasha enquired. "You have wished me dead. I have seen it in your eyes."

"That is not true," he replied. "What I have wished is that I were not part and parcel of this unpleasant bargain which you have made with Shamyl."

"You had to be an accessory to the crime," Natasha said lightly. "There was no-one else available."

Lord Athelstan pressed his lips together.

"Take what money you require," he said coldly. "I imagine you will find sufficient here."

Natasha was about to answer him when the door into the Sitting-room was opened and a servant announced:

"Her Excellency Baroness Walchian to see you, M'Lord."

Lord Athelstan turned round.

Coming into the room was an entrancing and attractive figure.

Wife of the Ambassador of Austria, Baroness Walchian had conquered Paris with her charm and her beauty, and for a short time Lord Athelstan had laid his heart at her feet.

She extended both hands to him now as

she seemed to glide across the room.

"D'Arcy!" she exclaimed. "How wonderful! How incredibly wonderful to find you here!"

"I had no idea, Kyril, that you were due in Tiflis," he replied.

"We arrived late last night and when I heard you were staying in the Palace I was ecstatic with delight — I was really!"

She looked up at him and Lord Athelstan thought she had not changed.

Her red hair which was characteristic of Viennese beauties glinted like fire in the light from the window.

Her eyes were green pools of mystery and her small, heart-shaped face was unforgettable to any man who had once seen it.

Lord Athelstan kissed both the Baroness's hands.

Then as if he suddenly remembered Natasha was there he said:

"May I present, Your Excellency, Prince Akbar of Sharpura, who is travelling with me to England?"

"I heard you had a guest," the Baroness smiled and held out her hand to Natasha.

"I am delighted to meet Your Highness!"

Natasha made no effort to touch the outstretched hand but raising her own pressed them together in the traditional Indian greeting.

"I have always longed to visit your beautiful country," the Baroness said.

She walked towards Natasha to seat herself on the sofa just vacated by Lord Athelstan and added:

"You must tell me all about it."

She gave Natasha a glance which would have sent any young man into a transport of delight.

"Tell me why you are here," Lord Athelstan said quickly to divert the Baroness's attention.

"Franz is on his way to Teheran," the Baroness explained. "For a visit — not an appointment — and from there we return to Rome."

She looked at Lord Athelstan.

"You are just as handsome as I remembered, *mon ami*."

"And you, if it is possible, are even more beautiful," Lord Athelstan replied.

As he spoke he was conscious of feeling a surge of anger at the hint of amusement in Natasha's eyes.

He wondered irritably why she did not leave the room. She must be well aware that her presence was not required.

"I tried to see you this morning," the Baroness said, "for I do not wish to miss a moment when we might be together; but I learnt you had gone with Prince David to meet the dreaded Tartars."

"That is true," Lord Athelstan said.

"Tell me about them," the Baroness said. "Are they as wildly attractive, as passionate and as handsome as they are reputed to be?"

Lord Athelstan did not reply and with a little light laugh the Baroness went on:

"Everyone is so sorry for the Princesses shut up with those Adonises! But I am told that it is the dream of every woman in Georgia to be swept up into the arms of some Tartar brave, flung over his saddle and carried away into the mountains."

Lord Athelstan knew without even looking at her that Natasha had stiffened at the Baroness's words, but he could not stop her vivacious chatter as she went on:

"I am sure our sympathy is wasted on Princess Anna. Doubtless by now she has found ample compensation for her captivity in the arms of Shamyl himself and as for the others . . ."

"It is not true! Such things, if they are said, are slanders!"

Natasha's voice seemed to ring out in the Sitting-room and the Baroness turned to look at her in astonishment.

There was no mistaking the fact that she was exceedingly angry and that there was a fire of fierce resentment in her dark eyes.

Lord Athelstan's diplomatic training brought him quickly to the rescue of what he realised might not only be an awkward moment but a very revealing one for the Baroness.

He gave Natasha a warning glance as he said:

"You must forgive His Highness, Kyril, for speaking so impetuously, but he accompanied me to Dargo-Vedin and was deeply distressed by the conditions under which the Princesses were living."

He realised as he spoke in a quiet, balanced tone that Natasha had regained her composure. But he knew that she had come near to betraying herself.

"I assure you," Lord Athelstan went on, "that the Princesses are very thin and emaciated. Their clothes are in rags and the cold they have experienced this long winter must have been almost insupportable."

"Do not tell me any more, D'Arcy," the Baroness begged, "you know I cannot bear to hear of horrors or listen to tales of unhappiness. I was simply repeating the Palace gossip and you can be sure I have heard all of it since I arrived."

Natasha rose to her feet.

"If you will excuse me, My Lord, I have some purchases to make and a servant is awaiting my instructions."

Once again the Baroness accorded to what she thought was a young Prince her most devastating and beguiling smile.

"We shall meet again tonight, Your Highness," she said, "and I shall look forward to it."

"Your Excellency is very gracious," Natasha replied.

She made an obeisance both to the Baroness and to Lord Athelstan and then she went from the Sitting-room.

"And now, D'Arcy, we are alone!" the Baroness said invitingly.

It was, Lord Athelstan knew, his cue to take up their association where it had left off.

But as he raised the Baroness's hand to his lips he was uncomfortably aware that Natasha was only the other side of one of the painted and gilt doors.

Could she be listening? He would not put it past her!

But even if she was not, he was aware that she was in the vicinity and that the fact that he found the Baroness attractive would amuse her.

"You are very stiff and formal," the Baroness said after a moment, "just as you used to be before I had melted some of that icy reserve which everyone believed had frozen your heart."

Her lips were very close to his and she asked softly:

"Shall we see, *mon cher,* if I can melt it once again? Have you really forgotten those nights in Paris?"

"I have never forgotten them!" Lord Athelstan answered in a low voice hoping that what he said could not be overheard.

"How long are you staying here?" the Baroness enquired.

"I leave tomorrow," Lord Athelstan replied.

He had already thought it would be wise to do so, but now he made an irrevocable decision that it was essential for him to leave as early as possible the next day.

"Then we have so little time," the Baroness said. "I shall however be resting between six and seven o'clock . . . I shall be . . . alone."

There was no need to say more and the Baroness's lips seemed to find Lord Athelstan's without his making any movement whatsoever.

As she touched him he knew that what had been between them was over.

Once she had been able to fire him as few

women had been able to do.

Once he had found her fluttering flirtations and the invitation in her eyes provocative; the pout of her lips irresistible; but suddenly the magic had vanished.

She belonged to his past and he was no longer interested.

With a little sigh the Baroness rose to her feet.

"I must leave you, D'Arcy," she said, "there are several people in the Palace that I have promised to visit, but I shall expect you at six o'clock. I am in the Empress's Suite. Any servant will tell you where it is."

Lord Athelstan had risen automatically and now he raised the Baroness's fingers to his lips and kissed them in a manner which seemed to please her.

Even as he did so he knew that she no longer excited him and he would make no effort to find the Empress's Suite at six o'clock.

"Until six, dear D'Arcy!" the Baroness said. "I know that we shall find again even in the short time available all the enchantment and the wonder which made us so happy together in Paris."

She laughed softly.

"I know that beneath that dry, diplomatic exterior there lies a very passionate and a very wonderful lover!"

She touched his cheek with her hand and then, her crinoline swaying like a flower in the wind, she moved across the room and had gone before he could reach the door to open it for her.

He stood staring after her, thinking as he did so how easily the fires of yesterday could be extinguished so that not even their embers remained.

Then he heard the door on the other side of the Sitting-room open and Natasha came in.

He had only to look at her face to know how angry she was.

"How dare she!" she said in a voice vibrant with emotion. "How dare that woman — that friend of yours — defame Princess Anna and the rest of us!"

Lord Athelstan did not speak and she went on:

"She obviously judges everybody else by her own standards! Her nights in Paris were hardly comparable to the nights when we lay shivering in the bitter cold with nothing but a worn blanket and our rags to cover us."

She paused to ask aggressively:

"Why did you not tell her how little food we had to eat? How we were persecuted and

126

made to suffer by the Imam's chief wife? And how even the servants vented their spite on us?"

She paused as if waiting for an answer and Lord Athelstan said:

"I am sorry that she should have spoken like that, but you cannot be so naïve as not to realise that women in this sort of place have romantic notions about the Tartars."

"Romantic!" Natasha ejaculated.

"There are stories that have been told and repeated all down the years," Lord Athelstan tried to explain. "It is inevitable with men who are so good-looking and so masculine."

"But surely you could have told the Baroness that what she was repeating was untrue?" Natasha insisted in an accusing tone.

"How do you know I did not do so?" Lord Athelstan asked.

"I heard what you said," Natasha answered. "It amused me to learn that after all you are not entirely made of granite!"

"I have always considered it very ill-bred to listen at keyholes," Lord Athelstan said scathingly.

"And certainly un-feminine!" Natasha added.

She was obviously unrepentant concerning what seemed to Lord Athelstan quite inexcusable behaviour.

After a moment he said:

"May I suggest that until we leave the Palace you should be a little more careful than you were just now? If you do betray yourself, it is not only I who will suffer but also your brother."

Natasha walked away to stand at the window, looking out onto the garden below.

"I realise I was indiscreet," she said, "but she made me so furiously angry. How dare that woman, who has always been wrapped in silks and satins and protected from cold winds, talk as if we had gone out on an amorous expedition with those barbarians?"

"You have suffered — I am not denying that," Lord Athelstan said, "but you had better restrain your anger until we are clear of Russian territory."

"What you are really suggesting is that I should keep my Arabian Nights tales for the Harem," Natasha flashed at him. "So you think the fat concubines will want to listen to me, or are you suggesting I should regale the Sultan himself with our sufferings?"

"I am suggesting nothing!" Lord Athelstan answered angrily. "I do not wish to think of you or your future. All I am concerned with is the present."

"And yourself!" Natasha said scornfully.

"As you say — myself!" Lord Athelstan replied.

He turned and walked into his bed-room leaving Natasha alone in the Sitting-room.

He had definitely made up his mind that he would not visit the Baroness at the time appointed.

But when six o'clock came she sent her own maid to the Suite to fetch him.

"His Excellency Baron Walchian requests the honour of Your Lordship's company," the maid said.

She spoke in French and was obviously a Parisian who, Lord Athelstan guessed, was responsible for making the Baroness the best-dressed diplomat's wife in the whole of Europe.

"*His* Excellency?" he asked, accentuating the pronoun.

"*Monsieur le Baron* wishes to see you, M'Lord."

It was impossible in the circumstances for Lord Athelstan to refuse, and he rose to his feet to follow the French maid just as Natasha entered the room.

She did not speak but she raised her eyebrows at the sight of the Frenchwoman and he knew exactly what she was thinking.

'It is none of her business!' Lord Athelstan told himself as he walked along the wide, exquisitely decorated corridors.

At the same time the fact that he knew she was criticising him made him feel that his decision to visit Kyril might have been precipitate.

He had found her very amusing and without doubt one of the most attractive women with whom he had ever been infatuated.

There had been many women in Lord Athelstan's life.

In fact women pursued him relentlessly, but he was very fastidious and only a few of those who offered their favours all too generously evoked any response from what the Baroness had rightly called his 'frozen heart'.

He had thought often enough that actually his heart was never engaged when he pursued his amatory adventures.

He would desire a woman, he would find her fascinating and he was often attracted to the point when he would wish to see her again and again.

But he knew, if he was honest, he had never really been in love.

Kyril was one of the few women to whom he had been attracted for quite a long time. Usually the flame of his desire burnt itself out quickly.

Then Lord Athelstan would grow more reserved and more detached than ever, and the mere fact that he was indifferent to them would drive more and more women almost mad in their efforts to ensnare him.

Kyril's charm made her shine like a light even amongst the beauties that thronged Paris and made it the gayest city in the world.

It was almost impossible to believe there could be so many beautiful, extravagant and alluring women in one place, and yet, as far as Lord Athelstan was concerned, he found Kyril eclipsed them all.

She was not only intensely feminine, which he liked, and more passionate than any woman he had ever known, she was also intelligent and knowledgeable on a variety of subjects in which he was interested.

She had, too, a puckish sense of humour which could at times be spiteful, but which always amused him.

Even in the midst of their lovemaking he would find himself laughing at something she said, but even so when she was making love Kyril would make her lover believe that he was a King among men and there had never been anyone like him.

All men like being flattered and Lord Athelstan was no exception to the rule, but

Kyril did it with subtlety to a point where he found himself believing all she told him and in consequence having a greater conceit of himself than he had before.

He wondered now as he approached her Suite whether what he had suspected when she touched his lips a short time ago was true and their attraction for each other had really gone.

Where she was concerned he was not sure.

He had the feeling she did in fact find him, as she had in the past, someone who excited her to the point where she was pre-pared to throw caution to the winds and brave any scandal which might result from their liaison.

The Baron was a much older man than his wife, and Lord Athelstan suspected he had long since given up worrying as to how Kyril behaved in private as long as she was cir-cumspect in public.

There had been moments in Paris when it had been Lord Athelstan who had applied the brake and made an effort to safeguard the Baroness's reputation.

Knowing Kyril's insistence on getting her own way Lord Athelstan expected when he reached the Empress's suite to find the Bar-oness alone.

To his surprise, however, His Excellency, the Austrian Ambassador was standing at his wife's side, looking resplendent in an array of decorations.

"Athelstan, my dear fellow, how nice to see you!" he exclaimed in his excellent English as Lord Athelstan was announced.

"I had no idea you were coming to Georgia," Lord Athelstan replied.

"As I expect Kyril has told you, we are on our way to stay with the Shah."

"I was with him two weeks ago," Lord Athelstan said.

Lord Athelstan realised this was all social chit-chat and of no particular consequence. Then the Baron glanced at the clock and said:

"You must forgive me, Athelstan, but I have an important meeting with the Viceroy which I am afraid will continue up until dinner-time. That is why I wanted a word with you now as I learn that you are leaving tomorrow morning."

"Yes, I must get home," Lord Athelstan said.

"I can understand that! I just wondered what sort of report you intend to make to the Queen about the Imam."

With an inward smile Lord Athelstan realised this was the reason why the Baron had wished to see him.

The Ambassador was attempting to find out, doubtless at the instigation of the Russians, whether England even at this late hour was prepared to support Shamyl and what advice Lord Athelstan intended to give the British Foreign Office.

Instead of prevaricating and evading the truth with well-turned diplomatic phrases Lord Athelstan decided to be honest.

"I think," he said slowly, "it is only a question of time, perhaps two or three years, before Shamyl has to acknowledge defeat!"

A sudden light in the Baron's eyes told Lord Athelstan that this was what he had hoped to hear.

It would be a feather in his cap if he could convey such information straight from Lord Athelstan's mouth to the ears of the Viceroy and through him to Field-Marshal Prince Bariatinsky.

Ironically, Lord Athelstan told himself, he had paid the Ambassador back for the times he had enjoyed with the Baron's wife in Paris.

Once gain the Baron looked at the clock.

"You must forgive me, my dear fellow," he said, "but I do not like to keep our host waiting. You know how punctilious he is in such matters."

"I do indeed," Lord Athelstan agreed.

"I shall see you at dinner," the Baron smiled.

He turned to his wife.

"Persuade His Lordship to come and stay with us in Rome," he said. "I think he would enjoy himself."

"I am sure he would!" the Baroness answered with a glance under her eye-lashes at Lord Athelstan.

Her husband kissed her hand and walked across the room.

He looked older than when Lord Athelstan had last seen him but he was still an impressive figure of a man.

The door shut behind him and Kyril held out her arms.

"You see, *mon cher,*" she said, "I was not deceiving you when you were told the Baron wished to see you."

She looked so mischievous that Lord Athelstan could not help laughing.

"How did you know I suspected the message?" he enquired.

"I had the feeling — and you know quite well, D'Arcy, that I can always, always rely on my feelings — that you did not intend to visit me this evening. Perhaps your young Prince put you off. Perhaps you have other and better loves than me."

There was just a touch of wistfulness in her voice which struck Lord Athelstan as pathetic.

Could it be that Kyril was beginning to doubt her own charms?

That seemed impossible, and yet women were unpredictable and none more so than Kyril herself.

He leant towards her but unexpectedly she rose to her feet and linked her arm in his.

"Come, I have something to show you."

They walked across the room and Lord Athelstan was conscious that she smelt of the same exotic fragrance which had haunted him when he had been her lover in Paris.

There was something unforgettable about it.

A scent which had remained with him long after he had left her.

She opened the door of a room, drew him inside, and only then did he realise it was her bed-room.

It had a magnificent canopied bed surmounted with the Voronzov crown which was supported by a number of gilded cupids.

Lord Athelstan heard the key turn in the lock behind him and then Kyril was in his arms.

"Oh, D'Arcy! D'Arcy!" she cried. "I have missed you! I have missed you more than I can ever say! Love me as you used to do! Love me and make me believe that we can be close again."

Automatically Lord Athelstan's arms went round her and she turned her heart-shaped face up to his. Her eyes were pleading with him and he knew it was impossible to refuse her.

So much of the past lay between them; so many hugs they had done and said together hovered like ghosts around them and were just as insubstantial.

It was an illusion, he knew, not only for himself but also for Kyril to imagine that their relationship could ever again be as it had been in the past. But for the moment they would both pretend!

They could try to fan the almost extinct embers into a small flame.

His mouth came down on hers and he lifted her in his arms.

It was more than an hour later that Lord Athelstan returned to his own suite.

He was glad to find that the Sitting-room was empty when he reached it. He rang the bell and ordered a bottle of champagne.

When it came he sat back in an arm-chair

drinking — for him — an unusual number of glasses, for he seldom drank alone.

He was conscious as he did so that he could still smell Kyril's fragrance. It hovered in his nostrils like a narcotic.

He believed he had made her happy, but he knew as far as he himself was concerned there was nothing more dead than a dead love-affair.

He had often thought of Kyril when he had been in India and even when he had been with other women, finding they did not measure up to her either in beauty, passion or charm.

She had always been the standard by which he judged every woman who had ever come into his life — and now there was no longer Kyril.

In fact there was no-one.

"I am thirty-five," he told himself, "it is time I settled down and produced an heir."

He thought of his great possessions in England and how he had always planned that sooner or later he would retire from the Diplomatic Service to look after his Estates, and play his part both in the County and in the House of Lords.

But he could not contemplate living at Athelstan Park alone.

It was too large, too imposing, and apart

from anything else, he needed a hostess.

Even as he thought of it he told himself he wanted much more than that.

He wanted a woman he loved; a woman who would be part of himself; a woman he would be proud to have as the mother of his children.

'I have almost left it too late!' he thought.

He realised that at his age he could not contemplate marrying some child who was just out of the school-room.

How could he tolerate an unfledged, tongue-tied *débutante* with whom he could have no intelligent conversation and who would doubtless giggle rather inanely at anything she did not understand?

The older women he knew were all married.

Those with whom he flirted and made love, like Kyril, had husbands who, whether complacent or jealous, were an insurmountable obstacle to marriage.

It seemed almost incredible that he knew no-one whom he could contemplate for a moment as his wife, but that was the truth.

He supposed there were few society families in which he would not be a welcome guest and who had not sent him invitations to house-parties, receptions, balls, assemblies, and every other sort of hospitality they extended to their friends.

But he could not remember amongst the whole lot of them one single, unattached woman whom he would consider worthy to step into his mother's shoes and take her place in his various houses.

"Yet it would be ridiculous to die a bachelor!" he said aloud.

He made up his mind that when he returned to England he would definitely make an effort to do something about his position.

The great hostesses of London would, he was quite certain, be only too glad to offer him their advice.

If the hostesses failed him there was always the Queen who, because she was so ecstatically happy with the Prince Consort, wished everyone else to enjoy the same connubial bliss.

But the Queen had married at twenty-one!

"How the devil could I put up with a girl of that age?" Lord Athelstan asked himself.

He felt himself shudder at the idea and knew that some idealistic streak in him rejected the thought of deliberately taking as a wife a member of a blue-blooded family to act as little more than a breeding-machine.

There were many men of his acquaintance who treated their wives in just such a manner.

They were left alone in the country producing baby after baby while their husbands enjoyed themselves in London. Keeping a mistress in one of the smart little villas in Regent's Park and frequenting the gay night-spots which increased year by year and which looked like making London a rival to the lurid attractions of Paris.

"I shall have to do something about it — and soon!" Lord Athelstan told himself.

The thought depressed him just as he felt depressed because Kyril had failed him, although he hoped she would not realise it.

Once he had believed that their desire for each other was more than just physical; that it had contained some of that elusive, half-spiritual ecstasy which Lord Athelstan believed all men sought but seldom found.

He faced the fact now that their union this evening had been entirely and completely physical, and because he knew her so well he was almost certain that Kyril would realise as he did that the magic had gone.

"What do I want? What the devil do I want of life or of women?" he asked himself.

He rose from the arm-chair and walked to the window.

Outside the sun was sinking in a blaze of

glory making the green fertile land in the valley seem almost a Paradise of beauty.

Lord Athelstan turned his face towards the sky.

Already there was the first faint translucent sable of the approaching night hanging over the distant mountains.

Then, as he looked, he saw flying directly above him the great outstretched wings of an eagle.

The King of birds seemed to hover in the light from the setting sun. There was something symbolic about him; something free and unrestrained; something omnipotent as if he was above the world and all its problems.

"That is what I want," Lord Athelstan told himself suddenly, "that is what I am seeking — to fly like an eagle!"

Then, almost as if he heard someone speak, the question was there:

"Alone?"

He turned from the window.

"What is the point," he asked almost savagely, "of seeking the impossible?"

Chapter Five

When Lord Athelstan left the Sitting-room Natasha turned and went back into her bedroom.

She did not know why but she felt angry at the thought of him making love to the Baroness.

She had taken a strong dislike to the beautiful Austrian because of the insinuations she had made about the Princess Anna and, incidentally, herself.

"How dare she think that we would enjoy being prisoners of Shamyl!" she raged. "How could she suggest that any decent woman would desire or submit to the embraces of an uncivilised Tartar?"

At the same time she was intelligent enough to admit there were women who would enjoy the excitement of being kidnapped by the mountaineers who were, if nothing else, exceedingly good-looking.

"That might also be said of Lord Athelstan," she told herself.

She had been so angry with him when at the Great Aôul he had refused to agree to take her with him to Constantinople that she had not thought of him as a man.

She had only known that he was deliberately putting obstacles in the way of her scheme to save her brother from being brought up as a Caucasian.

She had hated him with a violence that surprised even herself.

When having discovered her success in foisting himself upon her, he had raged at her, it had given her pleasure to know that she had broken through his reserve and incensed him to the point when he could barely control his temper.

She had, however, since they had arrived at the Palace heard a great deal about Lord Athelstan which had surprised her.

She had thought in her ignorance he was just a stupid Englishman, a nobleman who worked in the Diplomatic Service in a dilettante manner and had obtained his position thanks merely to his rank and breeding.

But she had heard the respect in the voices of those who spoke to and about Lord Athelstan and she could not attribute it solely to the fact that the Russians were anxious to be friendly with Great Britain.

The other guests in the Palace and the

Viceroy himself talked of Lord Athelstan in such glowing terms and praised him with such sincerity that, despite herself, Natasha was impressed.

She learnt of the journeys he had made all over the world on Britain's behalf and how his tact and charm had settled differences between Nations which everyone had been quite certain must end in war.

She was told that even the most stubborn and obstinate Rulers would become amenable in Lord Athelstan's hands, and there was no doubt that the Russians felt positively honoured by his presence.

She found herself looking at him with different eyes and now realised that he was exceedingly handsome.

Perhaps the most handsome man she had ever seen!

Even in St. Petersburg, she thought, where the Russians in their splendid uniforms caused every woman's heart to beat faster, he would not be overshadowed.

She discovered too that he was younger than she had at first supposed.

In her anger and resentment she had thought of him as middle-aged, someone too old in years to take a risk or relish an adventure.

Nothing in fact could have been further

from the truth, and finally she had to admit that Lord Athelstan's intelligence must be remarkable for the Viceroy to be so pleased to see him.

Natasha could not have stayed in Georgia without realising that Prince Voronzov, or 'The Accursed One' as he was called by the Murids, was a hero who was venerated to the point of worship.

Everything about him was on the same large scale as his Palace, and generations of noble ancestors all seemed to be embodied in one astute, ruthless, courageous and high-principled man.

Even to those who knew him well, the Prince was an enigmatic figure, haughty and reserved, and yet Natasha noticed that he unbent when he talked of Lord Athelstan.

The two men had, she realised, a great deal in common.

For one thing the Prince had been brought up in England. His father had voluntarily exiled himself from Russia as he dislike the Tzar, Paul I, and he spent those years in London. The present Prince therefore was one of the gay, raffish young Bucks who circled round the Prince Regent, later George IV.

When he returned to his own country he served the Tzar first as a soldier, then he was appointed Governor of New Russia and Bessarabia.

Here his brilliant administrative ability was discovered when he created a new Colony from what had been a wilderness.

In Odessa he introduced commerce, built harbours, hospitals, streets and colleges and, finally, employing an English architect, he created at Aloupkha on the Crimean shores one of the most fabulous, incredible, amazing Palaces the world had ever seen.

Rising sheer above the Black Sea the Prince's home was a fantasy which showed that beneath his cold exterior there was something irrepressibly romantic — perhaps a longing for the unobtainable which only a man like Lord Athelstan could understand.

In her bed-room Natasha walked about restlessly.

She tried to tell herself it was an impertinence and yet her thoughts could not help dwelling on Lord Athelstan and what he was doing at this very moment.

'How would he make love?' she wondered.

Would he be stiff and pompous as she had believed all Englishmen were, or was there a fire beneath that icy exterior that in her anger she had not sensed?

"How can he like such a woman?" she asked, and knew the question was unfair.

The Baroness was beautiful!

She was exquisitely dressed and Natasha had learnt from the gossip in the Palace that she was courted by men of every nationality wherever her husband's profession took them.

"She is frivolous and shallow!" Natasha said aloud and yet the criticism did not quite ring true.

On her dressing-table lay the dagger she had just purchased in the Bazaars and picking it up, she held it in her hand, testing the sharpness of the blade.

It was this weapon by which she would die.

It was a pretty ornament. Fashioned with the usual delicacy of the native craftsmen, the handle was set with coral and turquoises which in the East are always believed to be lucky.

Perhaps the dagger would bring her a swift and painless death.

She put it down and moved across the room to stand at the window as Lord Athelstan would do later, looking out over the green, lush valley.

She would never see it again.

In a very short time she would be enclosed

by the Harem walls and perhaps her only view through an ivory latticework would be of the Bosporus.

It seemed strange to think that her life was ending so quickly almost before it had begun, and yet, she told herself, she had no alternative.

It seemed a long way at the moment from her home near Warsaw and from the glories of St. Petersburg.

She had been brought up in Poland because her father and mother had lived on a small Estate there which had been left to them by a distant relative.

Natasha had not realised until she left it how free and unrestrained Poland was compared with Russia.

The nobles lived on their huge Estates in feudal magnificence, content to enjoy the life of a Princely Squire, riding across the plains on their thoroughbreds — ignoring the fact that they were for the moment beneath the Russian yoke.

Warsaw, with its old houses, ornamental fountains and narrow streets was considered the most fascinating Capital in all Europe, while those who lived there regarded themselves as Europeans.

It was in fact very cosmopolitan compared to St. Petersburg and was connected by a direct railway service to Paris.

There were smart shops, stylish dress-makers, while the very latest plays from France and Germany could be seen in the theatres.

What Natasha did not realise until she left Warsaw was that there was freedom of thought in her father's house which she was never to find again.

Her mother died when she was fourteen, and it had never struck her father that it was unusual to expect his daughter to take his wife's place in running the house or in playing hostess for him.

He was an extremely intelligent man; his friends were all intellectuals and they talked to Natasha as if she was grown up.

She had in fact had a very wide and en-lightening education. Her father had seen to that!

Because she learnt quickly and because she enjoyed learning, she absorbed far more than most girls, or, indeed, boys of the same age.

But it was the conversation of distin-guished men which had enlarged her hori-zons and made her seem much older than her years.

When her father died it had been a bitter blow, not only because she loved him, but because she now had to leave her home.

There could be no question of her and her small brother living there alone. The Tzarina heard of their plight and sent for them both to come to St. Petersburg.

Dimitri was more or less adopted by a delightful family who had sons of the same age.

He settled down immediately and there was no doubt he was extremely happy with two people whom he looked on, to all intents and purposes, as his parents.

Natasha was to live in the Winter Palace.

The Tzarina had two hundred ladies-in-waiting, all housed in the Palace.

Amongst them were several novices who, like Natasha, were to learn their duties before they were permitted to wear a cipher and crown in diamonds on their shoulders and a long red and gold train.

The first thing Natasha noticed in her new life was the excessive heat of the Palace, which seemed to stifle her after the life in the open air she had enjoyed in Poland.

The second was the fact that she soon learnt it was a breach of etiquette, and certainly unwise, to speak her mind.

She had, of course, heard her father and his friends in Warsaw talking about the despotism of the Tzar and the manner in which those who offended were punished by being sent to Siberia.

But she had not really believed it.

It had all seemed a strange fantasy invented by clever men to disparage those who had conquered them.

When she arrived at St. Petersburg she could not help noticing the contrast between the extravagant and unbelievable luxury of the Palaces and the ragged, half-starved creature she saw in the streets.

Because her father had taught her to be observant and not be afraid to criticise what she saw, Natasha looked at St. Petersburg not as a young, romantic girl might have done, but as an intelligent observer.

At first it was impossible not to be a little bemused and excited by the great colourful Royal Palaces — the Winter Palace a delicate green-white, the Youssoupov Palace reflected yellow in the Fontanka canal, and Voronzov Palace, which overlooked the Neva, was decorated in the family colours of crimson and white.

There were others in blue, lilac or pink, and their liveried servants were so colourful, so extravagantly garbed, that they appeared to be taking part in a theatrical performance.

In contrast there were the ragged Serfs

who could be flogged or killed by their masters, and the women and children who haunted the corners of the streets, with frightened eyes and skeleton-like hands begging for their bread.

Among the ladies-in-waiting at the Winter Palace was a young girl a little older than Natasha with whom she became friends.

Elizabeth was in love and, inevitably, she needed a confidante. Natasha filled the role admirably.

Their rooms were adjoining and they spent a great deal of the night sitting on each other's beds talking.

Natasha learnt that Ellico Orbeliani had declared his affection during a picnic in the summer and Elizabeth had fallen madly in love with him.

Letters were smuggled into the Palace from the Military Academy almost daily. They were touching, rather juvenile little notes. Although he was tall and good-looking, Natasha felt that Ellico was in many ways very young.

But to Elizabeth he was perfect!

He was her first love and she could talk of no-one else.

When they went to the Balls or Assemblies which took place every night in St. Petersburg she looked only for Ellico, and if he was not there the evening no longer held any interest for her.

Natasha, having spent her life with much older men and having as yet no knowledge of love or its effect on lovers, could not help feeling that both Elizabeth and Ellico were too young to be married.

But there was no doubt as to the sincerity of their affections.

She was surprised to find how little Elizabeth knew about running a house, how ignorant she was of the world outside the glittering, candle-lit Palaces and the artificial life led in them.

Had she any idea, Natasha asked herself, what it would be like to be the wife of a soldier? To accompany him to obscure, perhaps uncomfortable parts of Russia, or even to foreign countries?

She somehow could not visualise Elizabeth being anything but a pretty child moving like a flower over the Ball-room floor, or snatching a quick kiss amidst the orchids in the conservatory.

Nevertheless, the two young people loved each other although there was no question of Ellico speaking to Elizabeth's parents until he had passed out of the Military Academy.

Then disaster struck!

The Tzar was in one of his bad moods when he went to inspect the cadets.

He could be cruel to the point of brutality. He could be ruthless and completely unbalanced over something which concerned him personally.

The night before his inspection, a number of Cadets had enjoyed a roistering, noisy dinner at which they had all become extremely drunk.

It was the sort of evening in which all Russian Officers indulged, and perhaps it was because Ellico was so young that he could not stand the pace as well as his more experienced colleagues.

Whatever the reason, he was not only late on parade but he was also incorrectly dressed.

The Tzar made an example of him.

His uniform was stripped from him and he was sent to Siberia.

It seemed, when Natasha first heard of it, too fantastic to be true. But afterwards she told herself it was what she might have expected of a man who had shown himself to be as savage a despot as any Oriental, Mongol or Shah.

With Elizabeth sobbing in her arms, it was hard not to feel a horror she had never known before of a life where this sort of thing could happen.

Until this moment, Siberia had seemed to be a vague bogey-land to frighten criminals. Now it became a reality.

Because Elizabeth had to know what Ellico was suffering, Natasha also learnt where the deportees worked in caverns lit only by a lantern.

"Their boots are worn out during the months in which they march to their prison," the two girls were told. "When they reach Siberia they work bare-footed or they wrap their feet in straw tied with rags."

"Oh, Ellico! Ellico!" Elizabeth sobbed.

"They work until they collapse," their informant continued. "Then they are beaten back to consciousness by the whips of the Cossack Guards."

Elizabeth gave a scream of horror.

"They are forbidden to talk to each other. No prisoner may ever tell another why he has been deported. They merely work until they die!"

After this Natasha found she could not bear to look at the treasures made from the stones which came from the Siberian mines.

How much misery had a lovely vase of lapis lazuli cost? How many strokes of a Cossack's whip had produced the gleaming purple amethysts which circled a white neck?

She used to wish that she could walk about the Palace with her eyes closed, for every time she looked at the onyx and jade, the rose-quartz and the blue-john, she could no longer see their beauty but only the despair of the men who had quarried them and in whose eyes there was no longer any hope.

It was from learning about Ellico and trying to comfort a broken-hearted Elizabeth that she looked more closely into the whole structure of Russian every-day life.

She learnt little because it was dangerous to learn too much about the Secret Police.

There were whispers of the terrible abuses to which they subjected a helpless and unhappy people.

But even to speak of them made even the most distinguished of Russians lower their voices and glance over their shoulders, and soon Natasha found herself infected by the same insidious fear which ran like poison through every vein of Russian society.

It was one of the reasons why she had welcomed an invitation from Princess Anna Tchavtchavada, who was her god-mother, to go and stay with her in Georgia.

It was Natasha who had suggested that

she should bring with her her young brother Dimitri; for although he was happy she thought it would be good for him to get away for a short time from St. Petersburg.

She was well aware that Georgians were much freer and much happier than those who lived in the North.

It was fifty-four years earlier that the Kingdom of Georgia had been peacefully annexed to Russia.

Its peoples were not really Russian but a mixture of many races. They were happy, gay and smiling, and far enough from the North not to be overshadowed by the Secret Police or, indeed, the threat of Siberia.

Princess Anna had invited Natasha because she thought she would be a pleasant companion for her niece, Nina. But Natasha had found the young Princess uninteresting.

She seemed to be concerned only with her feminine attractions and not the least interested in politics or any of the social problems about which Natasha craved information as other girls might crave for sweetmeats.

Every day while she had been in St. Petersburg she had longed to be able to discuss what she saw and heard with her father.

Every night she had gone to bed wishing

that there was someone with whom she could speak frankly and who would explain to her why such cruelties should continue unchecked.

Conversation in the Great Aôul had not been at all interesting or intelligent.

It had been impossible for them to think of anything beyond their physical sufferings, the lack of air, and the difficulty of keeping out the cold with their inadequate clothing.

In any case, they could not converse coherently with so many people in one room, the screaming and whimpering of the children or, worse still, when they tried to play boisterously, and above all the unceasing complaints of the servants.

When things went wrong the servants just wailed, and while Princess Anna was unfailingly patient with them, finding their lack of control understandable, Natasha found herself extremely exasperated with them.

From the moment she had set off in her daring disguise under Lord Athelstan's involuntary protection, everything had changed.

There had been men to talk to, not only Lord Athelstan but also the Officers who had accompanied them, first to Vladikavkaz and then to Tiflis. And the Palace was full of men who reminded her of her father's friends.

She listened while they discussed the new scientific discoveries, when they talked of war and what new tactics could be employed to defeat Shamyl.

They argued about Persia and the Shah, about the Crimea and the British, Afghanistan and what appeared to be an imminent outbreak of war on the Indian frontier.

To Natasha it was like breathing fresh air after having been incarcerated in a dark cellar for years on end.

She felt herself coming alive again.

She joined in the conversation, remembering with great difficulty to assume what she called her 'Indian voice', and knew that those who listened to her were astonished that a young Rajput Prince should be so knowledgeable.

It was like drinking champagne and she knew that even with a 'sword of Damocles' in the shape of the Sultan hanging over her head she was happier than she had been for a long time.

What was more, although he undoubtedly was still annoyed with her, she was looking forward to travelling alone with Lord Athelstan to Constantinople.

The evening was gay and amusing and the conversation was very stimulating. There were fifty people to dinner, and an orchestra played in the great Salon.

Then, as Natasha was thinking it was time to go to bed she saw that Lord Athelstan was talking alone with the Baroness.

Wearing a gown which could only have come from Paris, she seemed to be pleading with him. Natasha fancied she was asking him to visit her again, perhaps when everyone else was asleep.

A wave of fury swept over her. She could not tolerate the knowledge that he should be so interested in the woman who had said such unkind things about the hostages.

A moment later Lord Athelstan kissed the Baroness's hand and came across the room.

"I think it time we retired," he said courteously to Natasha.

She did not answer, sure that she knew the reason why he wished to leave the rest of the Viceroy's guests.

Holding her chin high, her eyes dark and stormy, she preceded him up the magnificent carved staircase.

They reached their Sitting-room. The candles in the huge chandeliers had been extinguished, but those in the gilt sconces were glittering low.

Natasha turned to face Lord Athelstan.

"Good-night, My Lord," she said coldly. "I hope you enjoy yourself with your slanderous friend."

She saw him stiffen. Then he replied icily:

"That remark is out of character. No genuine Rajput Prince would be so tactless, insensitive or ill-bred as to speak in such a manner!"

"So you think I exemplify those faults!"

"It is regrettably obvious!"

"I am, My Lord, armoured against your aspersions as I am against the injudicious tongue of the Baroness. I merely dislike having to be associated, even remotely, with such a woman."

"And, apparently, with me!" Lord Athelstan added.

Natasha made an acquiescent movement with her hand.

"The remedy is quite simple," Lord Athelstan said, his voice like a whip-lash. "You can stop this masquerade or go on alone!"

With a start Natasha realised that she had walked into a trap.

It was her own fault. She had raged at Lord Athelstan impulsively, without thinking, driven by an emotional reaction she did not understand.

She turned away from him and stood for some seconds irresolute before a huge vase of lilies. Then in a low, strangled tone she said:

"I . . . am . . . sorry . . . I apologise."

Lord Athelstan did not answer and after a moment she went on:

"Please . . . let me . . . travel with you —"

He was about to make a scathing reply when, looking at her thin figure and her proud head surmounted by the brilliant turban, he paused.

There was something inexpressibly gallant about her. She was so young, so vulnerable, yet she had embarked on this crazy adventure.

She also — and Lord Athelstan was certain she had meant what she had said — was prepared to die at the end of it.

He suppressed the angry retort which had sprung to his lips and instead, gently, in a voice he had not used before, he asked:

"Shall we forget this small skirmish?"

There was a pause before Natasha answered:

"Are you . . . generous enough . . . to do that?"

She waited until, as he did not answer, she turned round to face him. He was looking at her and there was an expression on his face she did not understand. Then their eyes met.

Something strange and unaccountable passed between them. Natasha could not explain it. She only knew she felt suddenly breathless, as if there was a constriction in her throat.

For what seemed a long time they both stood very still before Lord Athelstan said:

"Good-night, Natasha!"

It was the first time he had ever used her Christian name. Then he went to his own Bed-room, leaving her alone.

The next day they started off very early in the morning.

Lord Athelstan's servants, whom he had sent direct from the Persian border to Tiflis with his heavier luggage, together with those who had accompanied him to Dargo-Vedin, made up a cavalcade of some twenty-five.

Everything was carried on horseback so that they could move more quickly.

Most travellers of Lord Athelstan's importance use carts and wagons and sometimes even camels to convey their luggage.

But Lord Athelstan insisted on pack-horses, and that all of them should be of a quality which would not cause him too much delay by going too slowly.

When they left the Palace behind, with its troops of crimson and white lackeys, Lord Athelstan said to Natasha with a smile:

"I think we would enjoy a gallop so that we can take the edge off our horses."

This was good reasoning. He and Natasha were mounted on the Kabarda stallions which had been a present from the Imam.

Owing to inactivity yesterday when they had been kept in their stables, they were now fidgeting to be off, bucking and rearing, and only two really experienced riders would have been able to hold them.

Lord Athelstan saw by her expression that Natasha was delighted at the suggestion, and a moment later they were riding ahead of the servants.

For Natasha it was a joy to know that she was astride a magnificent stallion. She had not ridden such a splendid animal since she left Poland.

After galloping for about two miles Lord Athelstan turned his horse back in the direction from which they had come. They only reined in when they were within sight again of the long file of riders and pack-horses led by Hawkins.

Natasha gave a deep sigh.

"That was wonderful!" she said. "If you only knew how much I have missed riding both while I was in the mountains and while I was in St. Petersburg."

"Did you not ride there?" Lord Athelstan asked in surprise.

"Oh, I rode," she answered scornfully, "tut-totting primly with the other ladies-in-waiting. They really prefer to drive!"

She gave him a little smile.

"It is considered correct, because the Tzar does so, to drive around the city in an open carriage, or a sleigh, depending on the time of year. The trouble is I never did like cities!"

"Neither do I!" Lord Athelstan agreed.

"You refused the Viceroy's escort today," Natasha said looking at the baggage-train.

"I thought we had seen enough of them," Lord Athelstan replied frankly. "And you make me nervous in case you forget either your Indian accent or that you are supposed to be a boy!"

"You are not very complimentary!" Natasha replied. "I thought my performance was faultless except for one little mistake."

"It was a mistake that might have cost you dear!" Lord Athelstan said seriously.

"I have already . . . apologised," Natasha answered.

He drew a deep breath.

"I feel as if I have been let out of school!"

She gave a little laugh.

"I suppose I should also apologise again for making you so apprehensive. What I found most difficult was not to reveal that I had been in the Palace before."

"Well, on the whole you gave a very convincing performance," Lord Athelstan said.

"Thank you, Sir!" she cried mischievously. "I never expected to hear words of appreciation from your lips!"

"I see you have made me into an ogre!" Lord Athelstan remarked with a faint smile of amusement.

"How could you expect me to think of you in any other way?" Natasha asked. "Considering how angry you have been with me ever since we have known each other!"

"You must admit I have had some provocation!"

"Perhaps," she agreed, "but I had expected you to have more sense of adventure. After all, a Diplomat should also be a buccaneer if he is to be successful."

"I have an idea that once again you are trying to needle me!" Lord Athelstan said. "You are a very persistent young woman, but if it pleases you I will make an effort to enjoy your adventure and, make no mistake, it is yours from now on!"

"I shall look forward to your effort," Natasha smiled.

"Then let me tell you something," Lord Athelstan said, "I have made arrangements for a messenger to bring us the latest bulletins concerning the exchange of hostages right up to the moment when we reach Constantinople."

His voice was more serious as he went on:

"There will be no point in your making this horrible and unnatural sacrifice if there is no reason for it."

"You mean if the negotiations broke down?" Natasha asked in a low voice. "Whatever I have to suffer, I could not bear that to happen."

Lord Athelstan did not speak and after a moment she went on:

"For one thing I do not think Princess Anna would live long. At one moment during the winter we feared for her life. She had a terrible cough, her hair began to fall out, and she was so exhausted that we had to do everything for her."

"I can understand what you suffered," Lord Athelstan said quietly.

He remembered the discomfort he had found in the Great Aôul, and, after all, he had been an honoured guest.

"What is more," Natasha went on, "do you realise that a prisoner's child, if orphaned, becomes by law what they call 'Allah's Own' and is therefore brought up in the Moslem faith?"

"No, I did not know that," Lord Athelstan answered.

"It would have meant that Princess Anna's children would have been taken from us immediately on her death and we would never have seen them again."

Natasha sighed.

"Princess Varvara often said she would wish to die so that she could be re-united with her husband, who had been killed in battle. But she had to live for her child's sake."

"I do understand what you have been through," Lord Athelstan said gently, "but I am sure the hostages will be exchanged. I only wish I could be as confident about your future."

Later that evening when they had encamped for the night in the shelter of a wood, Natasha said to Lord Athelstan:

"I would like you to tell me about the Sultan's Palace in Constantinople. I feel you must have been there."

"Yes, I have been received by the Sultan,"

Lord Athelstan replied. "Do you really wish me to speak of what lies ahead of you?"

"I would rather be fore-armed than surprised and frightened," Natasha answered quite seriously.

They had talked of many things while they were being served by Hawkins with an excellent meal, Lord Athelstan finding for the first time how knowledgeable Natasha was on subjects in which he would not have expected a woman to be interested.

It was a warm evening. The sun had disappeared from the sky, stars were coming out and there was a soft breeze to keep away the insects.

Hawkins had raised the sides of Lord Athelstan's tent and they could look out into the darkness. Near them the rest of the men had erected their tents and were seated around a bright fire.

The horses had been unsaddled and were cropping the grass. It was very quiet and peaceful.

Lord Athelstan thought it would destroy the beauty of the evening if they talked of what lay ahead, but Natasha had asked the question. He was determined to deflect her, if possible, from the course upon which she was set.

"Constantinople is the gate-way to the

East," he said, "the Capital of the Ottoman Empire and the home of the Caliph of the Faithful, the Shadow of the Prophet upon earth — the Sultan Abdul Aziz."

Natasha shivered.

"The Seraglio, or Harem," he went on, "has always remained a mystery and a legend. The word derived from the Arab *haram* meaning 'forbidden, unlawful'."

He saw Natasha was listening intently and he continued:

"When the Sultan rides abroad in his capital, he is surrounded by guards carrying large banners and pearl-fringed umbrellas, and waving ostrich-feather plumes to screen him from curious eyes."

He smiled as he went on:

"Foreign visitors like myself are given a magnificent robe before they approach the Sultan. When he received me he was seated on what looked like a gigantic four-poster bed of silver and gilt encrusted with precious stones."

Natasha could not help giving a little laugh.

"Were you impressed?" she asked.

"But of course," he replied. "It would have been most undiplomatic to be anything else!"

"Go on," she implored.

"Actually I saw very little apart from the main Reception-Rooms. But I noticed the Black Eunuchs who were on duty."

Again he thought Natasha shivered, but relentlessly he continued:

"The Chief Black Eunuch ranks with the Grand Vizier. His power is absolute. He alone has the right to speak directly to the Sultan."

He drew in his breath as he said:

"It is the Chief Eunuch whom you will have to placate and who will decide your fate one way or another."

"I understand," Natasha said in a low voice.

"I have always been told," Lord Athelstan continued, "that the Seraglio is a kind of huge nunnery whose religion is sin and whose God is the Sultan."

He added, and his voice was cynical:

"But those who imagine it to be just a place of unbridled licence have obviously been reading too many novelettes. I imagine the worst enemy is boredom."

"I imagine that, too," Natasha said. "All those women shut up together are bound to result in a great deal of envy, spite and jealousy."

"One can almost say the same of the Eunuchs because they are unnatural. They are ironically known as 'The Keeper of the

Rose' or 'The Guardian of Delights' but that certainly does not prevent them from using their hippopotamus-hide whips!"

His eyes were on Natasha as he spoke. She was looking out into the darkness.

'Her profile is perfect,' he thought.

There was no mistaking the pride in her aristocratic little nose and curve of her lips, nor the winged eye-brows above dark eyes which held now a look of horror.

"Could you bear," he asked quietly, "to be shut up day after day, week after week, year after year?"

"I am ready to die."

"I wonder if that will solve your problems," he said. "Perhaps you will have to come back to live again the life you have so carelessly expended long before you have paid the accumulated debts from your last existence."

She turned to look at him and he saw her eyes light up.

"You are talking of re-incarnation," she exclaimed. "Were you interested in it before you went to India?"

"I studied all Eastern religions when I was at Oxford," Lord Athelstan replied.

"My father had some books about it," Natasha said. "I have always wanted to know more."

"All I have is yours!" Lord Athelstan quoted, with a gesture of his hand.

Natasha gave a little laugh of sheer delight.

"Tell me everything you know!" she said.

"Impossible!" he replied. "If I talked all day and all night I could only begin to touch the tip of the ice-berg as far as Buddhism alone is concerned!"

Natasha put her arms on the table and cupped her face in her hands.

"If you only knew," she said, "how much I have wanted to meet someone who was really interested in the East."

"Why particularly?" Lord Athelstan enquired.

"The two things I have always wanted to do," Natasha replied, "are to visit India and China and to live in England."

"Surely a conflicting aim?"

"Not really," she replied. "I believe that the East can give solace to my soul, and the West — personified in England — all that I need physically, especially being able to think and speak freely."

"I think before we get too involved in the theoretical possibilities of re-incarnation," Lord Athelstan said, "you must tell me about yourself. I know very little about you."

"There is very little to learn," Natasha replied.

"Because you are very young?"

"Because I have done so little — in this life."

There was a little pause before the last three words.

"You really believe that you have lived before?" Lord Athelstan asked.

"Of course I have!" she answered. "So have you and so has everyone who is perceptive, intelligent, intuitive . . . Those qualities could only come with living and living fully, with learning, with understanding and with experiencing."

"I wonder if you are right," he said.

"Look at it this way —" Natasha began.

They were still arguing and discussing the subject when suddenly Lord Athelstan realised the rest of the camp was very quiet.

He looked out to see that while the fire was still burning, the men had long since gone to their tents or rolled themselves up in blankets with their heads on their saddles.

Everyone was asleep. Yet Natasha and he had been so interested in what they had had to say to each other that the hours had gone by unnoticed.

"You must go to bed," he said almost reluctantly. "We have a hard day's riding ahead of us tomorrow and I would not want you to be too tired."

"I will not be tired, My Lord," Natasha answered. "The way we have been talking tonight has given me a new impetus."

He looked at her with a smile in his eyes.

It was true, he thought.

She looked more alert and there was something radiant and sparkling about her that he had not noticed before.

"All the same," he said, "I think you need your sleep."

Even as he spoke he knew that she was thinking as he was, that she would have plenty of time to sleep once she was in the Sultan's Seraglio which was waiting for her at the end of their journey.

Waiting for her to pass through the four doors, two of wood and two of iron, which led to the Harem; through the four doors, with four great locks and past the Black Eunuch who held the keys.

"Good-night, My Lord," Natasha said.

She rose to her feet and he thought how slender she was and remembered the privations that had caused it. Then to his own surprise suddenly he found himself saying urgently:

"Natasha, do not do this thing! If Shamyl keeps your brother prisoner, then I will negotiate for his release. It will only be a question of money. However much he requires, I will pay the sum!"

Natasha's eyes went to his face and he saw there was an incredulous expression in them.

"You, My Lord? But why should you do that?"

"Because I cannot bear to think of any Christian woman in the power of the Sultan," Lord Athelstan answered. "You do not understand — and how can I tell you? — the humiliations and indignities to which a woman, whether she is termed his wife or his concubine, must submit herself before she is allowed in his presence."

He paused.

"They are instructed in the 'Arts of Love', but they are not the Arts known to the West or indeed anything understood by someone like yourself."

Natasha did not answer and he continued:

"It is not so much what you might suffer at the hands of the Sultan that perturbs me. With the hordes of women he keeps imprisoned it might be years before he chooses you. It is what you must learn in the meantime which appalls me. Nothing you have read or dreamt about could prepare you for that!"

He paused to say,

"A concubine, or a wife, approaches the Sultan on her knees and draws nearer to him, starting at his feet!"

His voice sharpened.

"Can you not understand the significance of that?"

"I have told you that I will die by my own hand," Natasha said.

"I wonder if when the time comes you will have the courage," Lord Athelstan questioned. "You will have no gun which would give a quick, clean death. Will you really have the determination or the strength to drive a dagger into the right place in your body so that you will die instantly? It is not an easy thing to do."

"I am aware of that," Natasha said sharply.

"And if you fail," Lord Athelstan said relentlessly, "you will be sewn alive into a weighted sack and drowned — an operation I understand is ritually performed by the *bistangi* — or garden boatmen — in the presence of the Black Eunuchs."

He saw Natasha was trembling and continued ruthlessly:

"It is very Russian to hold life cheap, but what else have any of us of any real worth? Just as a baby will fight to live when it is almost too weak to breathe, so I am asking you to live, Natasha, to fight for your existence."

"I cannot! Do you not understand? — I cannot go back on my word!" Natasha cried.

"A word given to a man who is a trickster and a charlatan when it comes to an exchange of hostages!" Lord Athelstan said harshly.

Then as Natasha did not speak he stormed:

"Very well! You have made your decision and I have no right to interfere with it. But let us make one thing quite clear: if, when we reach Batoum or Constantinople, the hostages have not been exchanged for Djemmal Eddin, I will not let you go on with this senseless sacrifice!"

He spoke so violently that Natasha looked at him in surprise.

"I shall take you back and damn the consequences!" he went on harshly. "Make no mistake about it, Natasha, I mean what I say!"

Chapter Six

They set off early the next morning as swiftly as was possible, but inevitably hampered by the pack-horses which were heavily laden.

The countryside was mountainous and wooded and the road to Batoum twisted round high-peaked hills and ran beside swift-moving streams.

It was very beautiful, but wild and at times the road, washed by the snows of winter, became little more than a track.

Lord Athelstan and Natasha were ahead of their baggage train when they saw coming towards them in a cloud of dust a rider moving at break-neck speed.

Instinctively they reined in their horses, wondering who the rider could be and aware that something must be amiss for the man to be travelling at such a pace.

He drew nearer and nearer, and now they could see he was middle-aged, conservatively dressed; and Natasha thought, in fact, that he looked as if he were a clerk or Civil Servant.

As he drew nearer he reined in his horse slightly but obviously did not intend to stop. As he drew alongside he shouted: "Tcherkess! Tcherkess!" and, spurring his horse, galloped on again at his original speed.

Natasha looked at Lord Athelstan apprehensively.

He had already grasped the situation and, turning back, gave a sharp order to Hawkins.

In a very few minutes the whole cavalcade had turned up a slight incline and into the depths of a thick wood.

Looking over his shoulder in the direction from which the man had come, Lord Athelstan said to Natasha as the last of the pack-horses disappeared into the shadow of the trees:

"Hurry! We must not be seen!"

She realised even better than he did how dangerous the Tcherkess could be.

Those who journeyed to Georgia by way of the Black Sea were always warned of the threat of marauding bands of Tcherkess.

After the Russian seizure of the coast they had been driven inland, but they still lurked in the wild countryside, a danger to travellers and ships which were not adequately protected.

Submerged rocks, mists and the unpredictable storms in the Black Sea resulted in a number of ships running aground or being split in two on the rocks.

When they were not protected by a Russian Man-o'-War, the Tcherkess looked on them as 'treasure-trove'.

They watched the whole coast from a chain of inland mountains and were always ready to ride down and snatch what they could from their Russian enemies.

They were a rough, murderous and cut-throat lot who were greatly feared and lived entirely by their wits and the proceeds of plunder.

Inside the wood Natasha dismounted, and one of Lord Athelstan's servants led her horse away to join the others which had been taken through the trees to a place where they would be not only unseen but also out of hearing.

Leaving three men to guard them, the rest came back to hide themselves behind the trees at the edge of the wood, their guns in their hands.

Natasha went to stand beside Lord Athelstan and he handed her one of his six-barrelled pistols.

No-one spoke, they only waited. Then in the distance they saw a great cloud of dust and realised the Tcherkess were approaching.

Nearly thirty of them, they were all tall, well-built men, each with a gun slung on his back and a silver-mounted knife in his belt.

They wore long, well-fitted coats and black, fur-bordered caps.

There was no doubt that their appearance was dashing, Natasha thought, but the expression on their faces was formidable.

They came nearer, riding swiftly, and Natasha hoped that they would pass by, still in pursuit of the man who had evaded them.

Then, when they reached the incline beneath the wood, they drew their horses to a standstill.

They started to talk and argue amongst themselves, laughing at a joke, but at the same time cruel and resolute in their demeanour.

They were obviously trying to decide whether they would go on or go back. Natasha could not help thinking how pleased they would be if they realised there was a greater prize and far more loot immediately at hand.

She looked along the line of Lord Athelstan's men, each standing behind a tree-trunk with his gun at the ready.

Their numbers were almost equal, but at

the same time the Tcherkess had a reputation for being crack shots, incredibly brave and afraid of nobody.

If it came to a battle it was doubtful who would be the victors. Either way there would doubtless be a great many wounded and perhaps a large number of dead.

She found herself holding her breath.

The Tcherkess were very near.

If they should become suspicious that they were being watched, if there should be the slightest noise to attract their attention, they would spring into action.

It only needed a whinny from a horse, the sound of a bridle being shaken, that a man should cough or even move.

The tension was intolerable. Suddenly Lord Athelstan found a very cold, frightened hand slipped into his.

Just for a moment he was still with surprise. Then his fingers tightened over Natasha's and felt hers pulsating in his like the movement of a bird which has been caught in a net.

Still they waited, still it was hard to breathe. Then the Tcherkess made up their minds.

With a shout not unlike a war-cry they rode back in the direction from which they had come.

There was the sound of their horses' hoofs galloping away; then there was only the cloud of dust which gradually disappeared over the horizon.

Natasha drew a deep breath which seemed to come from the very depths of her body.

The Tcherkess were gone and they were safe — at least for the moment!

"It is all right!" Lord Athelstan said smiling at her as he might have done to a child.

"They are savages!" Natasha said in a low voice.

"I have heard about them," Lord Athelstan replied. "We were lucky, very lucky that we were warned in time to hide from them."

He looked at his watch and found that it was just after noon. He told Hawkins they would rest for a short while so that the men could eat.

He walked a little further into the wood until he found a small clearing where he sat down on a fallen tree while Natasha seated herself on the mossy ground.

"Did you not encounter bandits and robbers on your journey through Persia?" she asked.

"I am sure there were many of them

lurking in the wild parts of the country," Lord Athelstan replied, "but the Shah sent with me a number of soldiers so that I was well protected."

"As the Viceroy would have done had you not refused his offer."

Lord Athelstan did not reply and after a moment she added:

"If anything had happened to us it would have been my fault!"

"I cannot allow you to blame yourself," Lord Athelstan answered. "I took the responsibility of going alone."

"Only because you were afraid that I might accidentally betray you," she said. "Now I feel ashamed."

"There is really no need for you to feel like that," he replied, "but I will admit it was a rather hair-raising moment! I was half-afraid that, like us, they would choose to shelter in the trees and then we should have had to fight!"

"I was . . . terrified!" Natasha said simply.

He remembered how her fingers had quivered in his and after a moment he remarked with a hint of amusement in his voice:

"I am glad to find that after all you can be feminine when it comes to danger!"

She gave a little laugh.

"Why, like all men, do you resent the fact that a woman should be able to fend for herself?"

"I do not think I resent it," Lord Athelstan said slowly, "it is just that I feel it natural that women should be protected and looked after by men. That, after all, is what nature intended. Animals fight for their mates, and a cock-bird will be on guard while the hen is on her nest."

Natasha gave a little sigh.

"I suppose really that is what all women want," she answered. "We have an urge for independence, but we know when it comes to brute-force that we must rely on the superior strength of a male."

"And yet you have refused to allow yourself to be protected!" Lord Athelstan said.

She knew he was querying once again what she had decided to do when they reached Constantinople.

She turned her face towards the wood and said very quietly:

"I must do what I think is right! It would be so easy to allow you to convince me that I am wrong. Please do not try. I could not sleep last night for remembering what you told me."

"You asked me for the truth," Lord Athelstan said.

"Yes, I know," Natasha answered, "and now I am more frightened than I was before!"

Lord Athelstan repressed an impulse to start the argument all over again, but he told himself it was unfair.

She was so young; so vulnerable.

He could only pray that something might happen before they reached Constantinople. Perhaps there would be no exchange of hostages.

It certainly seemed before he left Tiflis that negotiations were breaking down, in which case he would send her back with some plausible explanation as to why she was not with the others.

It all flashed through his mind, but before he could speak again Hawkins arrived with food and drink.

It was only intended to be a picnic luncheon, but even so it was delicious.

There were cold meats, fresh salad, pâté for which the Viceroy's chef was famous, fruit and cheese.

There was also a superlative white wine which had been provided from the Voronzov cellars and which tasted like liquid sunshine.

"That was very good!" Natasha said as they finished.

"You feel more at peace with the world?" Lord Athelstan asked.

"For the moment I do not feel so apprehensive."

Then she added:

"Perhaps that is not true! What I really want is for this journey to go on forever — for us never to come to the end of it."

She thought he was laughing at her and she said quickly:

"It would be boring for you, I know, but for me it would be an enchantment out of time. It would make life so much easier — if we could escape from time!"

She saw Lord Athelstan was listening and went on:

"Have you realised how it rules our lives? It is always time to go to bed, time to get up, time to leave something exciting one is doing because it is time to go somewhere else, time to grow old, and time to die."

"I think it is true that there is not enough time for the things one wants to do," Lord Athelstan agreed, "and too much time is demanded for things which are boring or part of one's duty."

"That is true," Natasha agreed.

"And now," he said rising to his feet with a smile, "it is time to go! We have quite a long way to travel and tonight I want to camp near Batoum because I feel it would be safer there."

Natasha did not answer. She was disappointed that they could not go on talking together.

Once again she thought how fascinating it was to be able to be alone with a man who was clever and intelligent; to talk to him as she had never been able to talk to anyone she had met in St. Petersburg.

She had the feeling that her father would have liked Lord Athelstan. They would have understood each other, for they had many things in common.

She could imagine Lord Athelstan at home on his country Estate.

There was something about him which told her he was a good landlord, generous and understanding to the people who worked for him.

It hurt her to think of what the Serfs suffered in Russia, the cruelties inflicted on many of them by their masters; the manner in which they were of no account as individuals, only a possession, bound to serve and obey without being allowed to have any personality of their own.

They rode on again, and now the sun was hot and the dust rose to settle as a grey film on their clothes, on the horses and even on their skins.

But Lord Athelstan had no intention of slackening the pace, and there was no respite or stop until they came within sight of Batoum.

The last part of their journey was hard going.

They had to climb the coastal mountains, find the Pass and then descend on the other side.

The Black Sea looked blue and tranquil, but its name was derived from the storms which could prove very dangerous to voyagers and were as unpredictable as any woman.

The winds in the Pass blew away a lot of the dust they had collected on the plains, but even so Natasha was glad when they finally camped at the foot of the mountains on a fertile green plateau bestrewn with wild flowers.

Here it was warm and protected from the wind and there was a stream flowing down the mountainside providing water for the horses and themselves.

Natasha's tent, which was part of the equipment she had brought from Shamyl, was small, comfortable and weatherproof, but nothing like the size or importance of Lord Athelstan's.

However, it was adequate for her needs, and when one of the servants brought her a bucket of water and a basin she washed herself completely before taking fresh clothes from a roll that had been carried on a horse's back.

She let down her hair and brushed it, then bound it again in a turquoise-blue turban which was the same colour as the turquoises in her dagger.

As she did so she wondered if the colour would be lucky for her.

'At least tonight I can talk with Lord Athelstan and forget what lies ahead,' she told herself.

And yet, like a dark cloud overshadowing everything she thought and did, there was always the horror of the Seraglio ahead.

Once she reached Constantinople she would leave behind everything that was familiar, to become the bride of the Sultan.

Because such thoughts were terrifying, Natasha deliberately shook herself free of them.

"I will not think of anything but today . . . just today!" she told herself.

Finally, when she was ready, she went from her own tent and into Lord Athelstan's.

He rose to greet her. As he did so there

was the sound of a horse outside and a man dressed in Cossack's uniform came hurrying through the camp, a letter in his hand.

Natasha knew it was one of the messengers who, Lord Athelstan had told her, would be bringing him information all the way to Constantinople as to what was happening about the exchange of hostages.

He opened the envelope the Cossack handed him and drew out a piece of paper.

He read it; then, turning to the Messenger, thanked him and told Hawkins to pay him.

It was a sum obviously considerably more than he had expected, and the Cossack's eyes glittered as he expressed his thanks before Hawkins took him away.

"What does it say?" Natasha asked.

Lord Athelstan's face was set and his voice unemotional as he replied:

"The terms have been agreed. The only hold-up is that Shamyl insists on having the roubles in silver and it is quite a large sum for the Prince to find and will take time."

"But otherwise the exchange will take place?" Natasha said.

"There appears to be no other difficulty," Lord Athelstan answered, "except that the Murids will count out the roubles one by one. This alone will take twenty-four hours!"

"They do not trust the Russians?" Natasha asked.

"I imagine they are suspicious that they might receive less than the agreed sum. This could cause a dispute during the exchange and provide an excuse for the opposing sides to start fighting."

"Yes, I can see that," Natasha said in a low voice.

She knew she should be elated at the news that Princess Anna and her family should be free.

Yet deep within herself she felt that a wild improbable hope which she could not control was disappearing like a tiny glimmer of light being extinguished in the darkness.

As if he knew her thoughts, Lord Athelstan held out a chair for her at the table and when she had seated herself ordered a servant to bring them wine.

"Let us be happy tonight," he said in a tone that many women had found beguiling. "There is still time for us to learn much more about each other."

"I am afraid you will only disapprove of what you learn about me," Natasha replied and wondered why her tone sounded so despondent.

"On the contrary," Lord Athelstan said, "what I learn about you interests and intrigues me. It is only what you do which evokes my disapproval."

Natasha sipping the wine felt as if it lifted a little of the fog that seemed to be closing in around her.

"What shall we talk about?" she asked.

"There has been no difficulty in finding a subject up to now," Lord Athelstan smiled.

It was true!

It had been so easy to talk to him. There was so much she wanted to know; so much only he could tell her.

As dinner progressed, which was even more delicious than that of the night before, she found he was opening new horizons for her, expanding ideas which had lain dormant inside her.

She felt as if he was stimulating her imagination until everything they said to one another had a strange enchantment.

"You are so wise — so clever!" she exclaimed impulsively. "Do you not ever feel lonely when you are travelling, and find you long for someone to be with you?"

"Of course I feel lonely," Lord Athelstan replied in his deep voice, "but I have never yet found anyone whom I wished to have permanently at my side. Perhaps that is why I enjoy travelling so much. There are always new discoveries either in people or places.

One never has time to get bored."

He paused to add:

"Perhaps the saddest thing is to find that what amused one yesterday has become stale and dull today."

As he spoke he thought of the Baroness.

It seemed incredible now that she had once meant so much to him. Yet if he was frank with himself he knew that one of his reasons for wishing to leave the Viceroy's Palace was to avoid having to see her any more.

No woman could bear to lose a man who had once loved her, and he was sure that sooner or later she would reproach him, once she realised he was no longer interested in her and she had lost the power to excite him.

He had wanted to run away from a scene which would have been unpleasant and in a way humiliating.

That he could attribute to Natasha his anxiety to leave had not really been a salve to his conscience.

He had known there were other reasons as well, and he thought that he must face them frankly and not deceive himself.

Aloud he said:

"One of the joys of life is that we can always go on learning; always go on making discoveries not only about other people but also about ourselves!"

"I think I understand," Natasha said.

"Prince David told me," Lord Athelstan went on, "that Djemmal Eddin's baggage consisted largely of books, atlases, paints, and drawing materials."

"Poor Djemmal Eddin!" Natasha exclaimed. "I doubt if he will be allowed to keep them."

"What do you mean?" Lord Athelstan asked.

"The Imam is very autocratic with his family. His youngest wife, Aminette, was upset that she was not allowed to wear rich clothing. I am sure the Imam will allow his son no reminders of the West except for those that he carries in his mind."

It seemed impossible, but Lord Athelstan suspected it was the truth.

"That is all I shall have," Natasha said in a low voice, "only what remains in my mind — memories of what you have told me and of our journey together."

She rose to her feet as she spoke as if she could not bear to talk of it any more.

It was already late and having said goodnight to Lord Athelstan she went to her own tent.

When she left him Lord Athelstan sat down at the table to pour himself another drink.

He thought of how they had conversed together and wondered if any other man had ever undertaken such a strange journey knowing that at the end he was to watch his companion condemn herself to a prison and to death.

He felt as if he must shake some sense into Natasha, and yet he knew that her will was as strong as his and that she was determined, whatever the cost to herself, to save her brother.

It was incredible that there should be so strong a sense of purpose in a girl so young, who had lived until now a quiet and sheltered existence.

"How can I make her understand what she faces in the hands of the Sultan?" Lord Athelstan asked himself despairingly.

Then he knew that whatever he might say, however black he might paint the picture, he would not be able to divert Natasha from her decision.

He picked up from the floor where it had fallen the message that had been brought to him about the exchange of hostages.

He could see so clearly the excitement which must be taking place at Hassif Yourt.

The terms had been agreed at last after all the arguments and all the prevarications.

Prince David would be thinking only of

the day when he would see his wife and children again, and Djemmal Eddin would be knowing, like Natasha, that he had reached the end of his journey.

All that was familiar, all that he loved, would be lost to him and there would be only the cold austerity of the mountains and a father of whom he was secretly somewhat ashamed.

It seemed to Lord Athelstan as if all this was happening in a second-rate, sensational Russian play.

The whole drama, which was in itself a tragedy, was too over-charged with emotion with the far-flung arm of fate dragging in undistinguished, unimportant lives to suffer beside the main characters.

If only Natasha had not gone to Georgia to stay with her god-mother! If only she had left her brother in St. Petersburg where he was happy!

There were so many coincidences, so many sub-plots, that it was difficult to disentangle them from the main action taking place between the Imam and the Russians.

"There is nothing I can do!" Lord Athelstan said.

There was a note of frustration and perhaps a touch of despair in his voice.

He decided to go to bed.

Then as he rose to his feet he heard the sound of horses arriving at the edge of the camp.

A moment later he saw in the light from the camp-fire an Officer in Russian uniform coming towards him escorted by Hawkins.

Behind him several soldiers were dismounting.

Lord Athelstan waited, wondering why soldiers should be visiting him at this hour of the night and what their arrival portended.

Hawkins brought the Officer to the tent and he stepped inside.

"I am Colonel Straganov, My Lord."

Lord Athelstan held out his hand.

"Good-evening, Colonel Straganov. This is a surprise!"

He saw that the Colonel was a man somewhat older than himself with a touch of grey hair above his ears.

He had a hard face with sharp, suspicious eyes.

He was the sort of man, Lord Athelstan thought, with whom he would have little in common.

"Will you sit down and have a glass of wine, Colonel?" he asked.

"Thank you. I should be glad of it," the Colonel replied. "We have come a long way."

Lord Athelstan raised his eyebrows and he said:

"From Vladikavkaz. I have been sent by Field-Marshal Prince Bariatinsky."

"Indeed!" Lord Athelstan answered, "and why has the Prince sent you to find me?"

Colonel Straganov sipped the glass of wine which Hawkins had poured out for him before he replied.

He spoke slowly choosing his words with care.

"The Field-Marshal has heard a rumour, although it may of course be untrue, that one of the hostages captured by Shamyl is under your protection."

"A hostage?" Lord Athelstan asked.

He was thinking quickly, realising that in the inevitable manner of the East a rumour had been started and had spread like wildfire to reach the ears of the Field-Marshal.

"I may tell you, My Lord," the Colonel went on, "that the rumour comes from Daghestan and has not of course been substantiated by our own people. I understand that when you stayed at Vladikavkaz you had a young Indian Prince with you."

"Yes that is right," Lord Athelstan said. "As a matter of fact he has now left me. He had to return to India unexpectedly and started home from Tiflis."

He raised his voice as he spoke, knowing that as Natasha's tent adjoined his, it would be quite simple for her to hear everything that he was saying.

He was taking a chance in saying that Prince Akbar was no longer with him, but he knew that if the Colonel had come from Vladikavkaz he would not have been in touch with Tiflis.

He would have come straight across country and therefore would not be in a position to know whether the supposed Prince had left the Palace in his company or not.

"The Field-Marshal was rather surprised that you should have taken an Indian Prince with you to Dargo-Vedin," the Colonel said after a moment.

"I had no choice in the matter," Lord Athelstan answered. "The Maharaja wished me to escort his son to England and I could hardly leave him sitting by the roadside while I visited Shamyl."

"No, of course not," the Colonel agreed. "I would, however, have liked to talk with him."

"Then I am afraid you will have to catch him up on the road to Teheran," Lord Athelstan answered lightly.

He refilled the Colonel's glass and his own as he said:

"I am sorry these rumours should have given you so much trouble."

"It is all in the day's work!" the Colonel replied. "At the same time you will not mind if my men look around your camp?"

Lord Athelstan stiffened.

"I am afraid, Colonel, you forget I claim diplomatic immunity. This camp is British and on principle I cannot allow searches or persecutions of any sort whether I have or have not anything to hide."

The dignity with which he spoke obviously impressed the Colonel.

"Of course, My Lord, if you feel like that about it I would not think of incommoding you. You will, I hope, allow me to rest a little before I continue my journey to Batoum? I am sure my men are already accepting the comfort of your fire."

"I hope they are!" Lord Athelstan said genially, "and I am delighted to offer you the hospitality of my tent."

He was well aware as he spoke that the Russians, while ostensibly being convivial with his men, would make every excuse to find out what they could.

It was obvious the Colonel had no desire to cause an international incident. At the same time, the Field-Marshal must have been fairly sure of his facts before he despatched such a senior Office on such a long journey.

He could only pray that Natasha, having heard the conversation, would disguise herself in some clever manner or contrive that no-one should enter her tent.

The Russians were experts at spying and he was quite certain that Colonel Straganov had brought with him well-trained men, picked for this particular mission.

They would be as astute and as skilful as the Secret Police. They would worm their way into every hole and corner in which they suspected something might be hidden.

He glanced towards the camp-fire and saw to his relief that most of his men had already retired for the night.

The Russians were being given drinks by Hawkins and two other men who had been with him ever since he had left India and whom he could trust not to gossip, however skilfully they were interrogated.

"I understand you found it a very arduous journey to reach Dargo-Vedin," Colonel Straganov said.

"It was certainly not a journey I would like to undertake very often," Lord Athelstan replied.

"And when you saw the Princesses did you not wish you could do something for them?" the Colonel persisted.

"I did indeed," Lord Athelstan answered. "But, as you will realise, there was nothing I could do, except to hope that the exchange of hostages would be effected with all possible speed. In fact I understand that will take place very shortly."

"We must hope so," the Colonel replied.

There was a pause and then he said:

"How do you imagine this rumour got about that one of the women had left Dargo-Vedin with you?"

Lord Athelstan shrugged his shoulders.

"The story-tellers in the Bazaars always have to produce a new tale to titillate the ears of their listeners, and what could be more romantic than that I should carry off a captive from under the Imam's nose?"

He laughed.

"It would have been a rather difficult thing to do with the great Shamyl accompanying us in person some way from Dargo-Vedin — an honour, I understand, accorded to few people."

"That is certainly true!" the Colonel agreed. "He has not been seen for years and he does not have many visitors."

"I am not surprised," Lord Athelstan answered. "His home is extremely uncomfortable."

He yawned and said:

"I hope you will forgive me, Colonel, if I retire to bed. It has been a long day getting here and tomorrow I have to find a ship to carry me to Constantinople."

"But of course," the Colonel replied, "I must not keep you up. As soon as my men are rested we will proceed on our journey."

"You must not think me inhospitable if I say I hope you will not stay long," Lord Athelstan said. "My men also are tired. It was very hot this afternoon and the climb up the mountain Pass was extremely exhausting."

"I understand," Colonel Straganov said. "At the same time, My Lord, you are quite certain the Field-Marshal was mistaken in paying any heed to this rumour?"

"My dear Colonel, do you really believe that I would wish to involve myself in a situation which concerns only Shamyl, who wants the return of his son, and Prince David, who awaits his wife and family?"

The Colonel did not answer and Lord Athelstan went on:

"I have made it a rule all my life not to take sides in local disputes. I represent Great Britain and am concerned only with her interests and with no others."

"Britain is not a friend of the Russians," the Colonel said ponderously.

"Unfortunately that is true for the moment," Lord Athelstan agreed.

He rose to his feet.

"As I have already said, Colonel, I would wish to retire. Please help yourself to wine, and I am sure that it will not be long before you are pressing on to Batoum."

The two men shook hands and Lord Athelstan lifted the curtain which separated the outer part of his tent from his Bed-room and passed through it.

Inside he stood for a moment wondering what he should do. Had he been wise in leaving the Colonel alone?

He thought it would show how unconcerned he was.

At the same time he was afraid that the Russians would be suspicious enough to force their way on some pretext or another into the other tents.

It was easy to trip over a rope and, in falling, clutch at the flap which would give way in their hands.

He could only trust and pray that Natasha would not be discovered.

This he knew was potentially a more dangerous situation than any they had encountered so far, and he could only hope that he was playing his rôle sensibly and disarmingly.

He had thought although he could not be sure, because the Colonel's grim face showed no emotion that he had convinced him that the charges were incorrect.

At the same time he was afraid. He was afraid both where Natasha was concerned and also for his own reputation.

There was however nothing he could do.

Natasha would have overheard what was said. Hawkins, although he must have been surprised at learning that the Prince had not accompanied them from Tiflis, would know that Lord Athelstan had a good reason for saying so and could be relied on to support him.

Slowly Lord Athelstan undressed.

He could hear the Colonel refill his glass in the outer part of the tent.

The Russians seated at the camp-fire must also have been drinking. Their voices were growing noisy and excited.

'They must be getting drunk!' Lord Athelstan thought.

Then he wondered if they were acting a part.

Was this the moment when they would knock over the tents or fall inside one accidentally and thus be able to see what it contained?

Putting on a silk robe which reached the

ground he pushed aside the curtain.

The Colonel looked up at his appearance, a glass in his hand.

"Your men sound very merry," Lord Athelstan said. "It will be hard to sleep when they are making so much noise."

"I must give them a chance to rest," the Colonel replied surlily. "As I have already told Your Lordship, we have come a long way."

"It hardly sounds to me as if they were resting!" Lord Athelstan remarked acidly.

As he spoke he saw a man rise from the camp-fire and stagger unsteadily towards Natasha's tent which was the nearest to him.

Just as Lord Athelstan had expected he might do, he fell over the ropes, reached out to clutch at the flap which covered the entrance of the tent and pulled it open.

The light from the fire revealed the inside.

There was a mattress on the ground, some luggage and a pile of cushions, but otherwise the tent was empty!

Lord Athelstan drew in a deep breath.

Then, for fear he might say more than would be expected in the circumstances, he said sharply to Colonel Straganov:

"I think your soldiers should be a little more careful!"

"I will tell them," the Colonel answered. "We shall be going shortly."

"Before they do any more damage, I hope!" Lord Athelstan retorted. "Goodnight, Colonel!"

He went back into his Bed-room. It had been difficult to prevent his voice showing his relief.

Natasha had been wise enough to get away. Doubtless she was hiding somewhere and would return once the soldiers were gone.

Wherever she might be, Lord Athelstan knew he dared not show any interest in her movements.

As he stood there thinking, the curtain was drawn aside and the Colonel looked in.

"I only wanted to apologise, My Lord," he said. "I am sorry that my men should get so drunk so quickly. It is just that we have been travelling all day without food and in those circumstances alcohol quickly goes to their heads."

"Yes, yes, of course!" Lord Athelstan replied. "I understand."

He knew that the Colonel was making his apologies only so that he could inspect the inside of his tent.

The Soldier's sharp eyes took in the pile of cushions, the travelling dressing-table which always accompanied Lord Athelstan wherever he went, the leather boxes which had contained his clothes and requisites for the night.

There was nowhere that anyone could possibly hide and the Colonel drew back.

"Good-night, My Lord! I hope we will not disturb you again."

"I too hope not!" Lord Athelstan replied with meaning.

He was so angry at the bare-faced intrusion that he could hardly bring himself to speak without letting the Colonel know how furious he was.

But he knew that would be a mistake.

Whatever happened, he must ignore the Russians' suspicions and pretend they did not exist.

To appear discomfited would only arouse them to further efforts, perhaps to search the neighbourhood of the camp, in which case they might find Natasha.

He heard the Colonel sit down again at the table.

The men's voices around the fire were growing quieter and he knew that having discovered nothing they were ceasing to pretend to be inebriated and getting ready for their departure.

'Damn them!' he thought, 'Once they

have gone I can look for Natasha.'

He blew out the lantern, took off his robe, threw it down and pulled back the blankets over the fine linen sheets with which Hawkins had covered his special mattress.

There were a number of his pillows filled with goose-feathers.

He pushed some of them aside. Then turning on his side he blew out the other lantern which stood beside his bed.

He would show the Colonel, he thought, that he was quite uninterested in anything the Russians might do. To ignore their behaviour would be more convincing than anything he could say.

He turned over to lie on his other side and as he did so felt something warm, soft and frightened lying beside him.

For a moment he was incredulous!

It could not be true!

Then he reached out and drew Natasha roughly into his arms.

Just for a moment he held her against him, then his mouth came down on hers.

Chapter Seven

At first Natasha was only conscious of the hardness of Lord Athelstan's lips and that they hurt her.

Then as his kiss became gentler and at the same time more demanding, more possessive, she felt a feeling of wonder and rapture seep over her.

He held her tighter still and then his lips were on her eyes, her cheeks and the softness of her neck. She quivered against him, no longer frightened but awakened by a strange sensation which she had not known existed.

It was a dry cough from the other side of the curtain that made them acutely aware that one sound, one murmur might betray them.

It seemed in some extraordinary way to intensify for Natasha the poignancy of the thrills that made her breath come quickly.

Lord Athelstan kissed her lips again and then he pulled her nightgown from her shoulder to kiss her bare skin.

Now he was tender.

She felt him move his lips over her neck, no longer being demanding and possessive. He touched her as a man might touch a flower, feeling the velvet of it sensuously against his mouth.

She felt more excited than she had ever felt in her life and at the same time she felt safe.

He was holding her, protecting her.

She was in his arms and she felt as if nothing in the world could hurt her now.

Suddenly a voice on the other side of the curtain made them jump.

"We've found nothing, honourable Colonel!" a man's voice said in Russian.

"Are you sure — quite sure?" the Colonel asked.

"We have searched the whole camp. It must have been a mistake!"

"Perhaps!" the Colonel said doubtfully.

There was the sound of him pushing back his chair and rising to his feet.

Both Lord Athelstan and Natasha were very still, listening intently.

"We will go!" the Colonel said.

"To Batoum, Sir?"

"No. We will start on our way back. The Field-Marshal wanted my report as soon as

I could bring it to him."

"Very good, Sir."

They heard the soldier go from the tent and give a command to the others waiting outside.

The sound of bridles jingling told them that the soldiers were mounting their horses.

The Colonel gave an exclamation expressive of frustration, then followed.

They listened to his footsteps moving away.

He spoke to Hawkins and, as they still waited breathlessly, there was the clatter of horses' hoofs moving first at a trot and then at a gallop into the distance.

It seemed to Natasha as if an eternity had elapsed while she had been unable to breathe.

Now she gave a deep sigh of relief, and as she did so Lord Athelstan sought her lips and kissed her again.

He kissed her until she felt the tent, the camp, the country around them had disappeared. It was as if he swept her up over the snow-capped mountains and into the sky until there was nothing left of the world and they were alone in a Paradise of their own.

At last he raised his head.

"My darling! My sweet!" he said unsteadily. "Once again we have escaped!"

"I knew I . . . would be . . . safe with . . . you!" she whispered.

"I was afraid — terribly afraid that you would not understand, or that someone would see you moving out of the camp."

"It was much . . . easier to come . . . here," Natasha answered, "and I knew that . . . you would . . . protect me."

"Do you think that is what I am doing?" he asked with a note of amusement in his voice.

She turned her face against his shoulder.

"I did not . . . know that a . . . kiss could be so . . . wonderful!"

"You have never been kissed before?"

"No."

"Perhaps I was meant to be the first. I too never knew either that a kiss could be like that."

"So . . . wonderful?" Natasha questioned.

"So perfect! Everything I always longed for and missed."

His lips touched her cheeks as if he re-assured himself that she was there and then he said:

"I have wanted you like this, with your hair falling over your shoulders."

He touched it as he spoke, feeling it soft as silk beneath his fingers, knowing it was so long that it would reach below her waist.

He took up a handful of it, kissed it, then swept it back from her face and kissed her lips and her ears.

"To-morrow I want to look at you," he said. "I want to see you as a woman, not as a boy!"

Natasha did not answer and after a moment he said as if he was speaking to himself:

"It sounds impossible, but I have an idea what we must do."

"What is it?" Natasha enquired.

"I will tell you in the morning. Now I ought to let you sleep."

"Do you want me to go back to my own . . . tent?"

Lord Athelstan gave a little laugh.

"Do you really think I would let you go? No, my darling, you must stay here with me. I cannot lose you. I cannot bear that you should be away from me!"

They both knew, although he did not say it, that they had so short a time together, perhaps only three more days, and then they would have to part forever.

As if the urgency of time impressed itself on Lord Athelstan, he began kissing Natasha again.

Now his lips were so demanding and passionate that they aroused a response in her and she kissed him back, her breath coming quickly, her body moving against his.

"I love you!" he said.

The words seemed to force themselves from between his lips.

She was still for a moment before she asked:

"Is that . . . true? Do you really . . . love me?"

"I have loved you ever since the first moment I saw you," he answered, "when I thought you were the most beautiful person I had ever seen. But when you raged at me, I thought I was angry with you, but it was really because I was appalled and furious at what you intended to do."

He paused and added:

"Besides I thought you hated me!"

"I believed I did!" Natasha admitted. "I wished you to do what I wanted, and because you objected I wanted to think of you as a . . . stupid, insensitive Englishman. Instead —"

She paused.

"Instead?" Lord Athelstan prompted.

"I found myself longing for you, wanting you, loving . . . you."

"Oh, my precious, my brave little love!" he cried and he kissed her until once again the world was lost and they were alone in an empty sky.

"You are like an eagle," she told him, her voice low and deep.

"Why do you say that?" he asked.

"You are so imperious . . . omnipotent . . . above the world!"

"That is what I have wanted to be," Lord Athelstan replied.

He remembered that moment when he had stood at the window in the Palace.

"An eagle is a 'king among birds'!" Natasha whispered.

"And he can be very lonely," Lord Athelstan replied, "unless there is another eagle with him — the one he loves!"

"I feel when you . . . kiss me that you . . . carry me away from the . . . world and into a . . . boundless sky."

"God knows that is what I want to do. Can I really make you forget everything but this?"

His mouth was on hers as he spoke.

She put her arm around his neck and drew him closer until she felt they were not two people, but one — and nothing could divide them.

Natasha must have dozed a little before dawn and when she opened her eyes she saw in the dim light which had percolated into the tent that Lord Athelstan was up and nearly dressed.

"Where are you going?" she asked. "It must be very early."

"I wish to see Hawkins," he answered, "but stay where you are. I will come back to you."

He put on his coat, took a brief glance at himself in the mirror which stood on his travelling dressing-table and passed through the curtain.

Natasha lay back against the pillows.

"Could any other man be as handsome, as alluring, as wonderful?" she asked herself.

She felt as if there were no words to describe him.

She only knew that because of her love for him she felt like a flower turning its face towards the sun.

It seemed unbelievable that she should have spent the night in his arms.

Yet when she thought of the events leading up to the moment when she had known there was nowhere else to hide except Lord Athelstan's bed, she felt it was part of fate and inevitable.

But she had never imagined in her most secret dreams that love could come so swiftly or so violently.

Elizabeth had told her what she felt for Ellico, but that had been merely a juvenile, immature emotion compared with what she felt for Lord Athelstan.

She knew her feeling for him had a depth and a sincerity which was quite unlike anything she had ever expected.

This was not the romantic feeling of a young girl for a handsome man.

It was something fundamental, something so much a part of her whole being, that she knew they belonged to each other, not only in this life but in many others.

All that was deep and Slav and mystic within Natasha was aroused to the point when because she loved Lord Athelstan she wished to pour out her heart and her soul at his feet.

This was love as it should be, not the flirtatious posturings of the Ball-room or the Conservatory, but a love without pretence, primitive in its passion.

A love that was in her very blood and from which there could be no escape.

She lay thinking of Lord Athelstan for a long time until the rising sun made the inside of the tent glow with a golden radiance.

When he pulled back the curtain to enter again it seemed to her as if he came in an aura of glory.

Her face was turned to his, her dark eyes seemed enormous and filled with happiness, her hair was streaming over her white shoulders.

"You are beautiful!" he exclaimed. "That is how I wanted to see you!"

He stood looking at her, realising that last night when she retired to bed she had washed away the dark powder and cream that she had put on her skin in order to disguise herself as an Indian Prince.

Now she was very pale and her skin had that translucent quality that reminded him of a pearl.

She was slim, but her breasts curved beneath the soft material of her nightgown, and when she smiled, her whole face was radiant with an expression that he had never seen before.

He looked at her until she dropped her eyes before his and murmured:

"You make me . . . feel . . . shy!"

"I adore you when you are shy!" he answered, "and may I say again, my sweet, I much prefer you as a woman rather than a man!"

"But I must go on disguising myself," she said, knowing that the note in his voice made her quiver.

"I cannot allow that," he replied. "I want

to look at you as you are!"

She raised her eyes again to his enquiringly.

Lord Athelstan sat down beside her on the mattress and took her hand in his.

"I intend to have you to myself — and as a woman."

"How is that possible?" Natasha enquired.

"I have told Hawkins to proceed at once to Batoum with most of the luggage and to hire a ship for our exclusive use which has neither a Russian nor a Turkish crew. There are always ships of all nations coming to Batoum. It should not be hard for him to find one."

Lord Athelstan paused and raised Natasha's hands to his lips as he said:

"He has left with us just enough of his picked men whom he can trust not to talk. The others he will dismiss at the Port and they will return home, most of them having to travel to Persia."

Natasha was listening intently as Lord Athelstan went on:

"Hawkins will also send back a carriage for you. You will step onto the ship as a woman and that is how you will remain until we reach . . . Constantinople."

He had said the dreaded word and for a

moment neither of them spoke, until he said quickly, as if he could not bear to think of what would happen when they got there:

"Go and dress. Have you anything to wear besides the Prince's clothes?"

"Yes, I have something in my luggage," Natasha replied.

Lord Athelstan bent forward and took her into his arms.

He kissed her gently, then rose to his feet.

"Breakfast will be ready when you are," he said.

She left the tent as she had come into it the night before, by slipping underneath the canvas.

In her own tent she saw that Hawkins had put water for her to wash.

Then she unpacked the rolled bundle which she had brought with her from Dargo-Vedin.

Breakfast was on the table and there was the smell of fragrant coffee when Natasha joined Lord Athelstan.

He looked up and was surprised to see she was wearing the costume of a Daghestan gentlewoman.

Loose flowered-silk trousers were almost hidden by a full-skirted, tight-waisted tunic with wide, flowing sleeves and elaborate fastenings of silver braid.

She was wearing a fine muslin veil around her head together with a coloured silk kerchief which accentuated the darkness of her hair and the clearness of her skin.

She looked very beautiful and very Oriental as she smiled at Lord Athelstan's surprise.

"Aminette, Shamyl's youngest wife, gave me this to wear when my disguise was no longer necessary," she explained.

"You look very lovely!" Lord Athelstan said and she saw the admiration in his eyes.

Natasha seated herself at the breakfast table and the servants came in with hot dishes.

They were obviously well-trained for they showed no surprise at her appearance. Lord Athelstan could not help wondering how many of them, including perhaps Hawkins, had known the Rajput Prince was a woman.

It was true that Hawkins had expressed no astonishment when Lord Athelstan had told him this morning that he was travelling with a lady.

Not that there was anything particularly unusual about that. But Hawkins must have realised last night, when he heard Lord Athelstan tell the Colonel that Prince Akbar had left them at Tiflis, that there was some reason for the lie.

Hawkins had been with him too long and was too well-trained to do anything except what he was told to do.

Lord Athelstan knew that just as he trusted Hawkins, Hawkins trusted him.

There was a camaraderie between them, after travelling so many miles together and in such different countries, that could never be expressed in terms of master and servant.

It was almost as if they were partners, and Lord Athelstan well knew that without Hawkins he would find his life very much more difficult and complicated.

They had finished their breakfast when Hawkins returned galloping back into the camp with an assurance which told Lord Athelstan clearly that his mission was successful.

He knew Hawkins as well as he knew himself, and there was no mistaking the slight jauntiness in his walk or the glint of triumph in his eyes when he succeeded in what he set out to do.

But his manner was quiet and respectful as he came to the side of the tent.

"Well, Hawkins?" Lord Athelstan asked, "what have you found?"

"I think it will be exactly what you require, My Lord, a Greek yacht, the *Corinth*, very luxurious and extremely comfortable!"

Hawkins paused to allow Lord Athelstan to appreciate the full significance of his words before he went on:

"Its owner has gone to Moscow, M'Lord, and the Captain is only too delighted to charter the yacht to you for what appears to me to be a quite reasonable sum."

"You have put the luggage on board, I imagine?" Lord Athelstan said.

He knew that in the circumstances Hawkins would think it quite unnecessary to ask his permission.

"I have, M'Lord, and the carriage for Her Ladyship should be here within a quarter of an hour."

"Thank you, Hawkins," Lord Athelstan said. "The men were pleased with what you gave them?"

"Delighted, M'Lord! I only hope the harpies hanging about Batoum don't get it all off them before they start on their journey home."

"They seemed a sensible lot," Lord Athelstan remarked.

"It's been a long journey, M'Lord, with no female companionship."

Without waiting for his master's reply Hawkins moved away to start packing up what was left of the camp.

Lord Athelstan looked at Natasha and smiled.

"As Hawkins says, it has been a long journey," he said quietly.

"But now you have . . . female . . . companionship," she replied.

Their eyes met and she knew there was no need for either of them to express their love in words.

She had never seen that look in Lord Athelstan's eyes before and she saw that it transformed his face, sweeping away the coldness which made him at times seem too reserved, too detached from ordinary people.

Now he looked much younger and there was an eagerness about him. It added to his attraction, making him, she thought, quite irresistible!

She had no idea how lovely she herself looked with her big eyes filling her face, her lips parted, and her breath coming a little quickly through them because of the intensity of her feelings.

"You are so beautiful!" Lord Athelstan said, "but I do not like your wearing clothes that have come from Daghestan. Amongst my luggage there are some things that I was given by the Shah and I will ask Hawkins to find them. I want to see you in them."

"I will wear anything you wish me to," Natasha answered.

As she spoke she heard the carriage approaching and they looked out to see a closed vehicle drawn by two horses coming along the dusty road which led to Batoum.

It turned round outside the tent, and now Hawkins and the other men were placing Natasha's tent and Lord Athelstan's luggage on the backs of what pack-horses remained.

"You go ahead, M'Lord," Hawkins said to Lord Athelstan. "I will meet you at the ship. It will not take long to dismantle your tent."

"Thank you, Hawkins," Lord Athelstan replied.

He helped Natasha into the carriage.

The coachman whipped up the horses and they set off, bumping slightly over the rough surface of the road.

Lord Athelstan took Natasha's hand in his.

"Does this still seem to you an adventure?" he asked.

"A very exciting one!" she replied. "It was clever of you to think of hiring a ship in which the sailors would not be Russians or Turks."

"I wanted to be alone with you without being afraid of prying eyes or gossiping

229

tongues," Lord Athelstan replied.

"That is what I want too," she answered. "It is only now it is over that I realise how afraid I have been that people might be suspicious of something I did or said."

Lord Athelstan smiled and she continued:

"I feel goose-pimples all over me at times when I think how nearly I betrayed myself in the Palace, and last night, when that Russian Colonel came, I thought there would be no escape."

Lord Athelstan's fingers tightened on hers as she said:

"You were very clever with him. Never once did you lie and yet you convinced him that he was mistaken!"

"It is always unwise to lie unnecessarily," Lord Athelstan replied.

He spoke absent-mindedly, as if he was thinking of something else.

Suddenly Natasha slipped her arm through his and put her head on his shoulder.

"If only our ship could carry us to the end of the world!" she said.

"Let us pretend for the moment that is what will happen," Lord Athelstan replied. "We must not spoil our time together by worrying about what lies ahead."

That was sensible, Natasha thought, but

she knew that every second she was with him however wonderful, however precious, there was always the dreadful feeling that she could never have it again.

The sands were running out.

It was however inexpressibly wonderful to know that she would be close to him, to feel his hand holding hers.

They reached Batoum and drove to the quay.

It was easy to recognise the *Corinth* because it looked so much smarter, more luxurious and more expensive than any other ship in sight.

The Captain was waiting to welcome them aboard, and when they inspected the vessel that Hawkins had chartered for them both Lord Athelstan and Natasha were delighted.

It had not been built very long and had the latest steam engine, besides two masts.

The cabins were fitted out in exquisite taste.

There were two master-cabins side by side and, what was extremely unusual, a bathroom opening out of each of them.

The one Natasha chose had jade green walls with a draped bed of coral silk.

It was so pretty and when she exclaimed at its loveliness the Captain replied:

"My mistress, who is very beautiful, is known to have the most exquisite taste in all

231

Athens! She personally designed the decorations in the *Corinth*!"

"They are certainly very lovely!" Natasha said.

The Captain was obviously pleased at her appreciation.

The second master-cabin was a more masculine room. The Saloon in white and gold had deep sofas upholstered in brocade and gilt mirrors which reflected the light from the portholes.

"It is fascinating!" Natasha exclaimed when the Captain had left and she and Lord Athelstan were alone.

"And so are you!" he answered and held out his arms.

She ran towards him and he kissed her as if they had been apart for a long time and he had missed her unbearably.

"Darling! Darling!" he murmured. "How can I tell you how much this means to me?"

"I think I understand," Natasha answered, "because when I am in your arms it is to me all the wonder of the world."

"Do you mean that?" he enquired.

"You know I . . . mean it!"

He held her tighter still, kissed her until her lips were warm and red and her eyes were shining like stars.

They only separated because Hawkins

had boarded the *Corinth* and the engines had started up.

There was so much to talk about, so much to discuss, that the hours seemed to slip past almost too quickly to be credible.

The food was Greek but very delicious.

The Chef had taken on fresh stores at Batoum and the owner of the yacht kept a good cellar.

Natasha had little idea what she ate or drank. She only knew it tasted like ambrosia and nectar because she was with Lord Athelstan.

Everything seemed touched with magic, and every second they were together her love for him seemed to intensify and grow more vivid.

On Lord Athelstan's instructions Hawkins unpacked the Shah's presents from Teheran.

Natasha found they included the most exquisite caftans in brocade, lamé and gauze, some of them embroidered with precious stones, and there were even some lined with sable.

There were scarves and muslins embroidered with real gold and silver thread, belts and slippers sparkling with gems of every colour.

When she came into the Saloon before

dinner Natasha was wearing a caftan of rose-pink silk embroidered with turquoises and pearls.

Her hair hung down her back to well below her waist and she wore a wreath of turquoises and pearls to match those on her caftan.

Her feet were encased in embroidered slippers which turned up a little at the toe.

She stood inside the door waiting for Lord Athelstan's approval.

"You look as if you had just stepped out of a fairy-tale," he said. "You are the Princess of Beauty and the Queen of my heart!"

Natasha gave a little laugh of sheer happiness and ran across the room towards him.

He held her close for a moment and kissed her forehead.

"I am afraid you might vanish!" he said. "I feel as if you belong to an ancient Persian manuscript rather than to the modern world!"

"How could you be so clever as to have such lovely things for me to wear?" she asked.

"The Shah was quite certain that if I had not a wife to wear them I would surely have a dozen mistresses who would appreciate such gifts!" Lord Athelstan answered.

"And . . . have you?"

He shook his head. "There is no-one! No-one in my life except you!"

"And I would . . . like to be your mistress," Natasha whispered.

He drew her to one of the sofas and sat down beside her.

"Do you really think," he asked, "that that is what I want of you? Natasha, will you marry me?"

She turned to look at him her eyes very wide as he went on:

"I have never, and this is the truth, my darling, never asked a woman to be my wife. I have never before met anyone with whom I felt I could be happy or who could take my mother's place."

He paused.

"Not until I found you!"

Natasha looked at him then she jumped to her feet.

"Please! Please!" she begged. "Do not . . . ask me. You know what the answer must be! I cannot . . . bear to say . . . it!"

"My precious heart, try to be sensible," Lord Athelstan pleaded. "How could it be possible, now that we love each other, for me to let you go to your death?"

"I have to! Can you not . . . understand? I have to!"

She turned to face him and he saw the tears in her eyes.

"I love you! I love you . . . desperately, with every nerve in my . . . body and with every . . . breath I draw!"

There was a throb in her voice but before he could speak she went on:

"But do you think either of us could spoil the love we have for each other or find any happiness together, if our lives were built on . . . dishonour? If the price we had to pay to be . . . together was my brother's . . . freedom?"

Lord Athelstan drew a deep breath. Then as he bent forward his eyes on the floor as if he could not bear to look at her Natasha ran to him and knelt down at his side.

"Let us be happy! Please, let us be happy these hours and days we have with each other," she said. "If we torture ourselves it will only spoil our memories and perhaps damage the perfection of our love."

She had put her hand on his knee as she pleaded with him, and his fingers closed over hers, crushing them almost bloodless.

"You are right!" he said with an effort. "I will try to forget what lies ahead, forget that all I want is that you should be my wife. But it will not be easy!"

"It will be . . . hard for me . . . too."

She lifted her face to his and he kissed her,

but without passion.

It was as if already the darkness of the future was encroaching upon them, to stifle them with its evil.

Lord Athelstan made an effort during dinner to amuse and interest Natasha, and because they could never talk together without stimulating each other's minds, it was easier than they had expected.

The Chef excelled himself with the excellence of the meal.

When they had finished they went up on deck to find a warm, starlit night, the waters of the Black Sea calm, phosphorus gleaming on the waves in their wake.

It was a night for romance, a night for lovers, and they stood for a long time under the stars before Lord Athelstan drew Natasha downstairs to their cabins.

She undressed and got into bed, sure in her mind that while the surroundings were very different from last night, he would still come to her.

When he opened the door of her cabin she was waiting and impulsively she held out her arms.

He sat down facing her then he took both her hands in his, kissing one after another each of her long fingers.

His lips lingered on the softness of her

palms and then the little blue veins on her wrists.

"I love you!" he said in his deep voice.

She felt herself vibrate to him as if there was music in the very tone of his voice.

Then he said:

"Listen to me, my darling; I have something to say to you."

"What is it?" she asked apprehensively.

"Nothing frightening," he replied quickly. "I just wanted to tell you that I cannot leave you alone when we have so little time together. I shall stay with you and hold you in my arms, as I did last night. But I will not make you mine as you were meant to be."

He drew in his breath.

"You shall go to the Seraglio pure and undefiled."

Natasha's fingers tightened on his and then she said in a low voice:

"But I want to be . . . yours! I want to . . . belong to you with my . . . body as I do already with my . . . mind and soul."

Lord Athelstan shook his head.

"Do you think I could live with myself afterwards," he asked, "if I thought you would suffer in any way because I had taken advantage of your love?"

It was easy to say such things, Natasha thought.

But at times during the night she thought that the flames that burned so furiously in both of them would sweep away Lord Athelstan's control and he would possess her as she wanted him to do.

Once he wound the long tresses of her hair around her neck and asked hoarsely:

"Shall I strangle you, my precious, so that no man shall ever look on you again? No man ever presume to touch you?"

Natasha knew then that he was driven almost to breaking-point and because she loved him unbearably she answered:

"No man shall ever . . . touch me but you . . . that I swear!"

"How can I think of you dead?" he asked.

"Do not think of it," she begged. "Just understand that our love will last for eternity. Even if we cannot see each other, I shall always be loving you! I shall always be somewhere, waiting for you until we meet again."

"I want you . . . now!" he cried fiercely.

Then he was kissing wildly and passionately her lips, her neck, her breasts until she could no longer think, she could only feel his violence sweep over her like a raging fire which threatened to consume them both.

"I want you! I want you! You are mine —

mine in the eyes of God!" Lord Athelstan
cried.

But the self-control he had exercised all
his life forced the fire to die down, and then
he was gentle and tender holding Natasha
close to him until she slept against his
shoulder.

Only when she awoke with a start, annoyed with herself because she had been un-
conscious for some of their precious time
together, did she find he was still awake.

He was looking down at her with an expression in his eyes which softened his
whole face.

"I had been . . . dreaming of you and . . .
you were . . . here all that . . . time!" Natasha
said, a little drowsily.

"You look very beautiful when you are
asleep."

"I want to be . . . beautiful for you."

"You are!" he answered. "At the same
time it would not matter to me how you
looked. I know there is something so spiri-
tual, so perfect in our love that it does not
depend on anything material — not even
beauty!"

That was true, Natasha thought. She
would love him if he were maimed or even
deformed.

She would love him if he was ill, or if he

could no longer speak and tell her how much she meant to him.

"We are so lucky . . . so marvellously lucky," she said, "to have found each other! Whether it is for a short or a long time we know that we are complete, no longer two people . . . but one!"

"That is true!"

He kissed her mouth slowly and lingeringly.

Then his arms tightened and it seemed to her as if he drew not only her heart but her very soul from between her lips and made them his.

"You are mine!" he cried. "Mine until there is no Heaven and no earth — mine beyond the confines of thought!"

Chapter Eight

They had two days and three nights together when they touched the stars and
Natasha held the moon in her arms.

They were happy as few people are privi-
leged to be happy, and it seemed as if the
wonder of their love glowed like a light
inside them, transforming their faces so that
they were hardly recognisable even to each
other.

There were no difficulties between them;
no lovers' tiffs; no moments when they felt
slighted or irritated. Only the wonder of
being together and a love which increased
hour by hour.

There were inevitably moments when
Lord Athelstan's decision not to possess
Natasha was hard to keep.

One evening after dinner was finished
they were sitting in the Saloon and he was
telling her of his travels and the interesting
people he had met when she asked:

"There must have been many women in

those different lands whom you loved and who loved you?"

"There were many women," he admitted, "but love, as you well know, my darling, is a very different thing!"

"Is it?" she asked.

He put his arms around her and drew her close. Then he lifted her chin and found her lips.

He kissed her slowly and possessively before he said quietly:

"This is love! It would be impossible for me to love you more than I do at this moment!"

"Are you sure of that?" she asked, half-teasingly.

He kissed her again, kissed her until he knew that not only her lips but her whole body responded to him and something wild and fiery gleamed in her eyes.

"Does that answer your question?" he enquired.

"Not completely," she replied. "Perhaps you have felt like this for other women and then awakened in the morning to find as you moved on to another city it was only a memory, a ghost you had left behind you."

She was really only teasing because she wanted to hear him tell her again and again how much he loved her. But he took her seriously.

"How can you ask such questions?" he demanded. "How can you believe for one moment that what we feel for each other can compare with what I have felt for other women or that I should ever forget you?"

His lips became more passionate, demanding, almost violent, so that he compelled her to echo the flame which was rising in him.

He raised his head to say:

"Tell me you love me! I want to hear you say it so that I am utterly and completely convinced that you could never feel for another man as you feel for me!"

"Why will you not let me . . . show you that my . . . love is . . . greater than anything else in the whole . . . world?" Natasha whispered. "More than . . . fear . . . more than . . . life!"

She paused and put her arms around his neck.

"Love me, my darling! Make me yours! Let me belong to you just once — so that we can both know that our love is perfect and that God meant us for each other!"

Her words inflamed Lord Athelstan. He kissed her until she was conscious of nothing but the fire burning on his lips.

Then he said in a voice deep and hoarse with passion:

"I desire you and my body aches for you until it is a torture to touch you and not make you mine!"

He looked down at her eye-lids heavy with the passion he had aroused in her and the softness of her lips.

"But because I love you, because my love is greater even than human need, I will leave you as you are, pure and perfect; a woman at whose feet I worship!"

He looked at her for a long moment. Then he rose to his feet and went from the Saloon and she knew that he had gone on deck to seek the coolness of the night air.

It was some time before he came back to her.

Natasha was in bed waiting for him a little apprehensively, looking fragile against the white pillows, with her dark hair falling over the sheets.

He came into the cabin and stood looking at her. Then he crossed to her side and lifted her hand to his lips.

"Forgive me, my darling!" he said, "but you try me too hard. I am only a man!"

"The most wonderful man in the world!" Natasha said softly.

"You understand?" he asked.

"I respect you and adore you," she answered. "Forgive me for being so weak. I

have not your . . . control over my . . . de-
sires."

It seemed to her that night as they lay together talking, with the starlight shining
through the uncurtained portholes, that
they were closer spiritually to each other
than they had ever been before.

At the same time they were both acutely
conscious that Constantinople was drawing
nearer and nearer.

Natasha prayed there would be a storm
which would delay their passage, but the
surface of the Black Sea was smooth.

Then in the early morning sunlight she
saw the skyline of Constantinople for the
first time.

Thousands of domes and minarets
gleamed golden in the sun.

There were the busy lanes of shipping, as
galleys, mahoons, battle-ships, vessels of
every type, were converging on or leaving
the Port.

The *Corinth* tied up alongside a quay, and
Natasha knew that Lord Athelstan had
made his plans so that they could be together until the last possible moment.

He ordered Hawkins to set up his tent
flying the Union Jack bravely at the harbour-
side.

It was away from the busy, heavily populated part of the Port; the City rose sheer above them. To the South, Natasha could see the Royal Palace set on its promontory looking across the strait towards Asia.

It seemed immense and she knew that she looked at the roofs of not only the Palace but the barracks, the stables, the kitchens, the prison, the torture-chambers, the Hall of the Circumcision, the pleasure-gardens and the Mosques, all of which housed thousands of souls to wait on the Sultan.

There were cypresses, dark and somehow menacing outside the battlemented walls, and to Natasha they appeared like grim sentinels.

She did not go up on deck but stood at the port-hole in her cabin looking out, knowing that in a short while she would have to say good-bye to Lord Athelstan.

She wondered how she could turn away and leave him.

She was to find that he equally could not face the moment of parting when he must watch her taken from him in a palanquin.

Hawkins had discovered there was an English Man-o'-War just a short distance from the *Corinth*, not tied up at the quay but anchored out in the river, the sailors coming backwards and forwards to the shore in row-boats.

On Lord Athelstan's order Hawkins went aboard H.M.S. *Victorious* and returned to say that the Captain would be deeply honoured to carry Lord Athelstan as his passenger to England.

The only difficulty was they were already behind schedule and he would wish to sail as soon as it was possible for His Lordship to come aboard.

It was as if this message made it easier for Lord Athelstan to go ahead with the preparations for Natasha to be carried to the Seraglio.

'What is the point,' he asked himself, 'of prolonging the agony, knowing we must eventually part?'

It was better to make a clean cut than to linger on, torturing themselves until the pain was unendurable.

Even at the last moment he had hoped there would be some chance of Natasha being saved because the hostages had not been exchanged. But Hawkins had gone into the city and come back with two pieces of news.

Lord Athelstan had known by his servant's face that it was not what he longed to hear.

"I learnt in the bazaars, M'Lord," Hawkins said, "that His Imperial Majesty the Tzar is dead."

"Dead?" Lord Athelstan ejaculated.

"Yes, M'Lord, but the Russians, I believe, are mourning him only officially; a great number are glad that his cruelties will no longer be continued."

Lord Athelstan waited. He knew that Hawkins had something else to tell him.

"The hostages have been exchanged, M'Lord!"

Lord Athelstan did not answer and Hawkins said quietly:

"I delivered your Lordship's message to the Seraglio."

There was evidence of this a short while later when three horsemen from the Sultan's special guard of Janissaries arrived at the yacht.

They informed Lord Athelstan that the Caliph of the Faithful, Sultan Abdul Aziz wished to greet the representative of Her Britannic Majesty, Queen Victoria, and thanked Lord Athelstan for his courtesy in bringing to him a present from Shamyl the Avar, Imam of Daghestan.

"A palanquin with an escort will collect the lady in question within an hour," Lord Athelstan was told. "In the meantime we have with us the clothes she must wear before entering the Seraglio."

They handed over an exquisitely painted

box with a gold lock and hinges.

When Natasha opened it in her cabin she saw the clothing in which she would be adorned as a member of the Harem.

She changed her caftan for the full crimson *Chalvari,* or full trousers, which showed beneath a gold damask robe with wide sleeves trailing almost to the ground.

It was buttoned with topazes and belted by a huge, wide girdle of precious stones, the clasp fashioned of enormous diamonds.

The robe, or *entari,* was cut very low and showed the transparent gauze of a chemise.

There were bracelets for her wrists set with precious stones and diamonds to wear in her hair attached to very fine gold chains.

Every time she moved the gems glittered and shimmered in the sun.

Also for her hair there was a large aigrette fastened by a brooch and fashioned to represent a bunch of flowers, made of rubies, emeralds, diamonds and pearls.

Over it all she wore a full muslin veil which must be fastened across her face to hide everything but her eyes — the traditional yashmak.

When she was ready she waited in her cabin. It seemed that all emotion had left her, and she was too numb with misery to feel anything but a blank despair.

The door opened and Lord Athelstan came to her.

She turned to look at him and their eyes said all that needed to be said between them. Already they were past words.

All night they had talked as, in the darkness, they had held each other close.

Now there was nothing left to be said.

He looked away from her.

"I have made arrangements that you will be collected from the tent so that we stand on British soil. The boat from the British ship will be waiting for me, and as you move away I too will leave. I cannot watch you go."

The pain in his voice made her long to put her arms around him.

"Everything has gone aboard," he went on, "with the exception of the tent and the carpet on which we shall stand."

"How soon . . . ?" Natasha asked through dry lips.

"Hawkins will tell us when the procession is sighted coming from the Seraglio. Then we must leave the yacht."

Natasha looked around her cabin.

"We have been so . . . happy here."

Lord Athelstan did not answer and she said:

"You will take . . . care of yourself, my darling? Remember . . . wherever you are . . .

you still . . . belong to me!"

"Do you think I could ever forget that?" he answered. "You will always be in my heart."

"I do not . . . wish you to feel . . . tied," Natasha said. "You must marry and have . . . children . . . an heir to inherit your . . . house and your . . . title."

"How can you think I could take another woman to be my wife?" Lord Athelstan enquired.

"This has been a . . . dream," Natasha replied, "a dream so . . . wonderful so . . . perfect that it is not . . . reality. You have to go on . . . living in this world, my darling. There is work for you to do . . . and you must not . . . fail those who look to you for . . . leadership."

Lord Athelstan drew in his breath and then he answered:

"What you are asking of me is impossible! Can a man who has once entered Heaven endure for the rest of his life the agonies of hell?"

"You have always been . . . brave," Natasha said softly.

"My darling — my love! How can I let you go!"

It was the cry of sheer, unbridled pain, but before Natasha could reply there came a knock at the cabin-door.

"The procession is in sight, M'Lord!"

The blood seemed to be drained both from Lord Athelstan's face and Natasha's.

They looked at each other.

Then drawing a deep breath and lifting her chin she opened the door and preceded him along the passage, up the companion-way and onto the deck.

She knew that the Greek sailors were looking at her with curious eyes as she appeared in Turkish costume, but she crossed the gang-plank and moved over the short grass towards Lord Athelstan's tent.

Raising her eyes she could see, as Hawkins had said, the procession coming down the hill from the Seraglio.

She could see the guards who escorted the huge red and gold palanquin in which she must travel.

They were led by a band playing the strange, tuneless music which always heralded the Sultan on his excursions in his capital.

There also seemed to be a great number of other personages all in colourful clothes with waving plumes in their turbans or dark faces which made Natasha guess they were the Black Eunuchs.

She moved into the shadow of the tent and stood on the Persian carpet, drawing her muslin veil across her face and fastening it with a little gold hook which held it in place.

Lord Athelstan joined her and she saw him for the first time wearing his gold-embroidered Diplomatic uniform with glinting decorations on his chest.

He looked resplendent, very dignified, and a complete contrast to the gaudy procession of Turks coming towards them down the hill.

Natasha looked at him, and, although her lips moved, no sound would come through them.

She was saying 'good-bye' with her heart, her soul, her whole body, and she knew that after all it would not be difficult to die.

She could not live without him! The little coral and turquoise-decorated dagger she had bought in Tiflis was hard against her breast.

'I will kill myself to-night!' she thought. 'There will be no point in waiting.'

Perhaps if God was merciful her spirit would be somewhere near Lord Athelstan as H.M.S. *Victorious* moved through the sea of Marmora and into the blue of the Mediterranean.

She knew by his pallor and by the white line that encircled his mouth that he was suffering as she had never seen a man suffer before.

She wanted to touch him but she did not dare.

She only knew that what was happening was a crucifixion for them both, but there was nothing they could do about it.

The procession came nearer and still nearer.

Suddenly there was the sound of galloping hoofs thundering over the dry wasteland on which they were standing.

Lord Athelstan turned his head in the direction of the sound and so did Hawkins. They saw a man approaching in a wild manner that proclaimed him a Cossack.

He drew up his horse sharply just as he reached the tent, pulling the animal back almost onto its haunches, and flung himself from the saddle.

He held out a rather crumpled white envelope to Lord Athelstan who accepted it automatically.

He knew full well what it contained. They had already learnt of the exchange of hostages.

Hawkins rewarded the Cossack, and the man, his white teeth shining as he smiled, flung himself back into the saddle.

He saluted and moved away as Lord Athelstan opened the envelope and drew out the piece of paper it contained:

On Thursday, March eleventh, 1855 Djemmal Eddin, son of Shamyl, the Avar, Imam of Daghestan and the sum of forty thousand roubles were exchanged for the hostages who had been held for eight months in captivity.

Those of Colonel Prince David Tchavtchavadze's household who were returned are listed below . . .

Lord Athelstan went on reading.

Then suddenly he gave a cry, a sound in which there appeared to be mingled both triumph and horror.

He pressed the paper into Natasha's hands and picked her up in his arms.

The procession was within a few yards of the tent when Lord Athelstan turned in the other direction.

He carried Natasha across the intervening space between the tent and the row-boat manned by British sailors which was held at the quayside awaiting him.

After one startled glance Hawkins followed them.

Lord Athelstan deposited Natasha into the boat, sprang in and the sailors cast off.

"What is . . . happening? What . . . are you . . . doing?" she asked in a frightened voice that was hardly above a whisper. "You cannot do . . . this! I . . . must go with . . . them!"

"Look at the list! Look at it!" Lord Athelstan cried in such a strange voice that it was difficult to recognise it. "I heard him say it and still it did not penetrate my mind. God! How could I have been such a fool?"

"What are you talking about? What has . . . happened?" Natasha asked.

Because he seemed to expect it of her, she opened with trembling fingers the crumpled paper he had thrust against her breast and stared at it.

The names were listed:

H.S.H. Princess Anna Tchavtchavada and her children, Prince Tamara, Prince Alexander, Princess Salome and Princess Marie

H.S.H. Princess Varvara Orbeliani and her son Prince George

H.S.H. Princess Nina Baratoff
Madame Drancy
Count Dimitri Melikov

The servants and their children are as follows . . .

Natasha gave a little cry and Lord Athelstan said, still in the tone he had used before:

"The Prince said in my presence that he
would not allow even the youngest of his
servants' children to be detained — but still
I did not realise it!"

There was so much self-accusation in his
voice that Natasha wanted to comfort him,
but they had reached the ship.

The sailors were waiting to help them up
the rope-ladder onto the deck.

She climbed up, and only when she was
helped aboard by a man wearing the uniform of a British Captain did she look back
to see the procession from the Seraglio
standing staring at them.

The band had ceased playing and they appeared utterly bewildered at what had occurred.

Lord Athelstan had climbed up behind
Natasha.

"Welcome aboard, M'Lord," the Captain
said.

Lord Athelstan held out his hand.

"Thank you, Captain Brownlow," he replied. "I should be grateful if we could put
to sea immediately!"

"That's exactly what I intend to do,
M'Lord!"

"Also I should be obliged if you could exercise your authority as Captain and marry me as soon as possible, to the Countess Natasha Melikov, whom I have brought with me."

The Captain's expression did not alter.

It might have been quite an everyday occurrence for a lady to come board dressed in a diaphanous oriental costume and that he should be asked to marry her to a member of the British nobility.

"It'll be a pleasure, M'Lord," he said. "The Admiral's cabin is ready for Your Lordship."

"Thank you," Lord Athelstan replied.

He put his arm around Natasha and helped her down the steep companionway, and an Officer showed them into the Admiral's cabin.

It was large, airy and well-furnished, but if it was austere after the luxury of the *Corinth* they did not notice.

They could only stand looking at each other as the door closed behind the Officer and they were alone.

Suddenly, as Lord Athelstan put his arms around Natasha, she burst into tears.

"My darling! My precious! It is all right! It is over!" he said. "But I will never forgive myself for not believing that Prince David would get his way!"

He drew her closer.

"I might have known," he said as if to himself, "that Shamyl would somehow convince his Murids that money was not important, and in forgoing the larger ransom, they saved their souls!"

Natasha was crying against his shoulder. He put up his hand to draw the jewelled brooch from her hair and with it the muslin veil. He threw them both to the floor.

"Do not cry!" he pleaded. "I have never known you cry. You have been so brave, my beloved — so marvellously, unbelievably brave, and now I will make you forget your suffering."

"I am . . . crying because I . . . am so . . . happy!" Natasha sobbed. "I thought I would lose . . . you . . . now we can be . . . together!"

Lord Athelstan drew a deep breath; then, very gently, he put his fingers under her chin and turned her face up to his.

The tears were wet on her cheeks and her eyes were filled with them, but she was smiling and he thought he had never seen her look so beautiful.

"The future is all ours, my precious!"

"We can . . . fly like . . . eagles!" she answered, but her voice broke on the words.

Then Lord Athelstan's lips were on hers,

kissing her wildly, frantically, desperately like a man who has come back from the grave.

He drew her closer and still closer.

They were in the sky, high above the world, omnipotent, undefeatable and together.

Neither of them heard the Captain come into the cabin with a prayer-book in his hand.

About the Author

Barbara Cartland, who sadly died in May 2000 at the age of nearly ninety-nine, was the world's most famous romantic novelist. She wrote 723 books in her lifetime, with worldwide sales of over one billion copies and her books were translated into thirty-six different languages.

As well as romantic novels, she wrote historical biographies, six autobiographies, theatrical plays, books of advice on life, love, vitamins and cookery. She also found time to be a political speaker and television and radio personality.

She wrote her first book at the age of twenty-one and this was called *Jigsaw*. It became an immediate bestseller and sold 100,000 copies in hardback and was translated into six different languages. She wrote continuously throughout her life, writing bestsellers for an astonishing seventy-six years. Her books have always been immensely popular in the United States, where in 1976 her current books were at numbers one and two in the B. Dalton bestsellers list, a feat never achieved before or since by any author.

Barbara Cartland became a legend in her own lifetime and will be remembered for her wonderful romantic novels, so loved by her millions of readers throughout the world.

Her books will always be treasured for their moral message, her pure and innocent heroines, her good-looking and dashing heroes and above all her belief that the power of love is more important than anything else in everyone's life.